Giants
IN THE EARTH

THE METHUSELAH CHRONICLES
-BOOK ONE-

T. B. Thornton, Th.M.

First published in 2012. Revised edition published in 2023

Printed in the United States of America

Publishing services by Selah Publishing Group, LLC, Tennessee. The views expressed or implied in this work do not necessarily reflect those of Selah Publishing Group.

ISBN: 978-1-58930-285-3
Library of Congress Control Number: 2012913082

Dedication

This book is dedicated to my loving wife, Sharon. It would never have been written without her constant love, encouragement, and understanding.

Foreword

I GREW UP IN A SMALL AGRICULTURAL TOWN IN SOUTHWEST Florida, where my family attended a small Southern Baptist church. I was always taught that the Bible was the infallible word of God and, consequentially, everything in life was to be seen through that prism of understanding. I was taught this in Sunday school, Vacation Bible School, church services, and home, where that fact was never questioned.

However, while attending public school in that same small town, those convictions started to be challenged in science classes when I was introduced to the theory of evolution. I was always fascinated by science, and because I was also taught to respect the authority of my teachers, I couldn't understand how the Bible and the theory of evolution could both be true.

The Bible teaches that everything, including humans, was created in six literal days. However, the theory of evolution espouses that the earth and all we see evolved over several millions of years. I was raised to believe in one thing and taught in school to believe in another. I found this to be extremely confusing.

When I would ask my teachers about this, they would tell me, "What the Bible teaches is fine for learning how to live a moral life, but the story of creation was just that; a story. Besides that, all you have to do is look in your science book and you will see the proof that the theory of evolution is true. There is page after page of scientific proof that everything has evolved to the point where it is today. The Bible doesn't give you proof for anything it says. It just tells you stories."

What my teachers said made sense to me. Why would they lie to me? Why would my science book state these things as facts if they weren't true? I didn't understand what they would be gaining from telling me lies. After all, I was taught to trust them. However, this left me with a feeling of guilt. If I believed what my teachers were saying, I felt as if I were turning my back on God and calling Him a liar. This was terribly troubling.

I was fifteen when I made an appointment with Pastor Yates and sat in his office. I was always impressed by his faith and how it was evinced in his life. If anyone could settle this problem, it would be him. Therefore, I decided to ask him about it.

I was immediately struck by the sheer volume of books on his shelves when I entered his office. My idea that he was the right man to ask was reinforced by the thought that he had read all of them. I thought he must be a walking encyclopedia of theological knowledge, so I asked my question without hesitation.

"Pastor Yates, how can the Bible be true when there is so much proof for the theory of evolution?" His eyes got big as I looked at him, waiting on an answer. He thought for a moment, forming a steeple with his fingers. He looked me in the eye and appeared to be sizing me up. Then, he took a deep breath and asked me a question.

"Why do you think they call it the 'theory' of evolution?"

I had never thought about that before, and I didn't have a good answer for him. My teachers had always stated the theory as a fact and did it in a way that left no room for question. They always seemed so sure about it.

I answered him the only way I could. "I don't know."

He asked me another question. "Exactly what proof do they have for their assertions about evolution?"

I thought about that for a minute before answering him. "Well, my science books have these pictures that show the evolution of man from apes. They have found all these skeletons that they say are the links between the apes and humans." I thought I had him there.

He smiled at me and asked me another question. "How many of those skeletons that they say prove their theories have been found to be fakes?"

I wasn't ready for that one. "Fakes? My science books don't say anything about any of them being faked. Where did you get that?"

He looked at me in that kindly, pastorly way and softly spoke. "I suggest that you study a bit deeper into these things before you believe what your science books say. There are some books on this subject that you should read. I think you will find them very interesting." He then turned and brought down a few books from his shelves.

I wasn't satisfied yet. I had a few more critical questions I was sure Pastor Yates wouldn't have an answer to. "Why would my science books teach me something they knew wasn't true? Why would they fake the proof? What would they gain from doing that?"

"Money." He answered a lot quicker than I thought he would. He continued, "You see, those scientists get a lot of money if they make a great discovery that is said to be the 'missing link' between apes and humans. They also get a lot of recognition for those discoveries. Like most sins, it all boils down to money and power."

Our discussion lasted another hour before he had to leave for another appointment. He didn't know the answer to some of my more specific questions, but I was genuinely impressed by what I learned that day. The most glaring thing about it was that I had always been raised in a Bible-believing church, yet this was the first time I had ever heard these things. It was the first time I had ever considered that my textbooks may not be telling me the truth.

That conversation and my studies of evolution and creation sciences since then have opened my eyes to many things taught in America's public school systems. There are countless cases of half-truths, frauds, and outright lies that our children are being taught about evolution. My reason for telling you this is not to list them all here for you. I aim to make you aware of it and, hopefully, cause you to want to study these things for yourself.

Also, I think it is essential that you understand I wrote this book from the standpoint that the Bible is the infallible word of God. Some of the things written in the story may seem fantastical and unlikely, but I assure you, it is all based on scripture.

Admittedly, the time period for the setting proved problematic when looking for references. This book is set in the time between creation and the flood of Noah. There just aren't many reference books that describe this time. In fact, I only found two that I believe are reliable enough to use.

The first is, of course, the Bible. As stated before, it is true from cover to cover. However, the only part of the Bible that deals explicitly with this time period is Genesis, chapters 1 thru 6. But other sections were used for describing certain animals that are not seen in today's world, or at least are not the same today as they were then. The Book of Job, for example, was instrumental in this effort.

The second reference was the Book of Enoch. For the uninitiated, the Book of Enoch is believed by many to have actually been written by Enoch himself and passed down to Noah to be preserved on the ark at the time of the flood. If true, that would make it the oldest book in existence. It is a fascinating book that reads a lot like the Book of Revelation. In fact, the messages contained in the book seem to be written for the people living in the "last days."

Please understand that I do not consider the Book of Enoch to be the infallible word of God as I do the Bible. I am quite aware of the problems associated with some of the theology in that book. In fact, certain sections within the Book of Enoch are known as the "corrupted text." In these sections, there is a clear break between what is Biblically correct and what is not. These sections were added to the book much later by someone trying to use them for their own advantage.

With this in mind, I only used the Book of Enoch for the purposes of background and minor storylines. This book's theological statements are based solely on the Bible.

I would also like to take this opportunity to define a few terms and explain a few facts about the pre-flood earth that many people may not know. It will be helpful to the reader and will aid in forming a better mental picture of what you are reading.

First, the only unit of measure that we have any record of for that time period is the "cubit." A cubit is believed to be roughly the distance from a man's elbow to the tip of his fingers; in other words, about a foot and a half.

Second, no references to time (minutes, hours, etc.) are found in this book other than days and the occasional mention of where the sun may be in the sky. This is because our modern minutes and hours were probably not used in those times, and I thought it would sound wrong for the characters to use those terms.

Third, "mists" that water the vegetation are mentioned a few times. This is because the Bible states plainly that before the flood, it had never rained on the earth and that a constant mist watered everything. The climate at that time was much like what could best be described as a greenhouse. There are a few fascinating theories about why that is. I recommend looking at what many creation scientists say on this subject. You will find it most interesting.

Fourth, you will notice that no one in this book, including the animals, eats meat. Their diets consisted of fruits and vegetables only. This is because the Lord didn't tell anyone that eating meat was acceptable until after the flood. As with the previous point, this also makes for a fascinating study.

In conclusion, I have three hopes for the reader.

One, I hope you have as much fun reading this story as I did writing it.

Two, I hope your interest is sparked in learning more about the time period of the setting, the animals mentioned within, and the wonders of the Lord's creation.

Three, and most importantly, I hope that this book helps you see God differently than you may be used to, and through it, some may come to know His Son, Jesus, as their Savior.

Although Jesus, at least the way we know of Him, wasn't yet born during the time of Methuselah, He is mentioned several times in this book. See if you can find Him for yourself.

— T. B. Thornton, Th.M

Chapter 1

Year since creation: 663

THE TRAINING COMPLEX WITHIN THE WALLED CITY OF ENOCIA was alive with the sounds of clashing bronze. There were forty rows of what Azazel called "soldiers" in the large, square sparring area. Each row was made up of thirty of these soldiers. Each held one of these new tools that Azazel had called "swords," and a deflecting tool called a "shield." This was all still very strange to Tubal-Cain, who was standing on the platform overlooking the training grounds. He had discovered this new metal, bronze, forty years ago. Until twenty-five years ago, he had only used it for making farming tools that had aided the farmers of the area in the hard work of turning the soil and making mounds and trenches that helped the vegetables grow better. He had felt good about being able to help his neighbors while also making a good profit.

These days, however, he seemed to be in a different sort of business altogether. This new business was, according to Azazel, called "war." Azazel, a "Son of God," as he had called himself, told Tubal-Cain that war would be a most profitable venture for "the man who controlled the metals." Tubal-Cain wasn't sure how much this strange being could be trusted, but he had not, to his knowledge, misled him so far.

War had been profitable, but there was another side of this new business with which he wasn't entirely comfortable. The purposes of his farm implements had been straightforward and easy to understand, but these strange new tools of war were only made for one purpose that he could see; hurting and killing. Azazel had said that the purpose of these weapons wasn't primarily to hurt and kill but to intimidate one's enemy into giving in to your will to avoid being hurt or killed. Seeing what one of these swords could do, as in a demonstration given by Azazel, was a strong deterrent to one's unwillingness to yield.

Azazel called a meeting of the city leaders to demonstrate the effectiveness of these new tools. He asked one of the livestock raisers to bring him a large bull. He paid the man for the bull and told everyone to watch closely as he approached the unsuspecting creature. With his back to the neck of the bull, he said, "This is how easy it is to use these new weapons." In one swift motion, he turned and swiped down through the poor creature's neck as if cutting through a dry reed. The men of the city watched with awe as the beast's head slid to the ground, followed a few moments later by the twitching remainder of the body. To a man, all were impressed by the demonstration and were more than a little disturbed by how easy it was to destroy a life.

Afterward, the city leaders discussed what they had witnessed among themselves before calling the forum back together with Azazel to question him. "Azazel," started Mehujael, Tubal-Cain's great-grandfather, "What you have shown us today is truly impressive, but what purpose would it serve to be able to take a life with such ease? We are farmers and sellers of wares. We have good lives here and do not find much need of such violence."

"I realize," Azazel answered, "that you have good lives here. I can see that you have gotten by until now without such things. However, I am looking around your city today and asking you this; do you truly have all you deserve?" He gave that a moment to settle before continuing. "I have seen the cities to your north. They enjoy the same river that feeds your city, the river with which you quench your children's thirst. Do you know what is done in that river before it flows into your fair city? I have seen them bathe in it and then send their filth on to you. Do you Enocians not deserve the best for your children? These new weapons can make that all change!" said Azazel holding his sword high above his head. "They show you disrespect by dirtying your river, but they will most definitely respect the power of this sword when wielded by the skilled hands of your well-trained soldiers. Then, you Enocians, with the mere mention of your name, will strike fear into any who would dare to disrespect you again!

"You have, until now, allowed the tent dwellers to your east to share your grazing lands. Have they given you any compensation for this privilege? Have they even offered? You have allowed them to intimidate your men because of their superior size and strength due to their rugged work. They have been allowed to come into your city and take your sisters and daughters for their wives. This only so they can treat them harshly and force them to live like animals alongside their wild sheep and oxen." Azazel let that seep into their hearts. He could sense the anger and pride welling up in them.

"No more, men of Enocia! No more do you have to take these injustices from these people of no respect! I will teach you all you need to know to be experts in the art of war, and you will not be trampled upon ever again. Your children will drink and play in clean water without worrying about what others have done in it before it gets to you. You will be given just compensation for the use of your pasturelands. Your animals will have the best of the grasslands, and those wild men to the east will settle for what you give them to feed their wild and sickly animals. The city of Enocia will have the respect of its neighbors. If not, its neighbors shall have the sword of the Enocians to contend with!"

It was quite a stirring sight as Azazel gave this rousing speech with that gleaming sword overhead and the bull's blood still visible on the blade. He was indeed an imposing figure standing at four and a half cubits. He was well-built, had dark features, inky black hair, and a well-trimmed beard and mustache. His face was long and thin, and his eyes were nearly as inky black as was his hair. One could hardly look into those eyes without an overwhelming urge to give in to his every wish.

The city leaders, who didn't want to appear weak in protecting their subjects, fell ▨▨▨▨▨▨ and backed the new war movement authored by this charismatic stranger. All Azazel asked for his services were the hands of two of the city's virgins. This was agreed to right away and without any qualms.

In the twenty-five years since, there have been many changes in Enocia. What used to be an open city with friendly people had become a walled city of people who feel they deserve the best or nothing. They have minimal regard for what anyone else wants. The peace of this place has given way to strife between neighbors.

The people of Enocia wanted the respect of their neighboring cities. Azazel had said that they could get it with the sword. What they hadn't counted on was that the people of those neighboring cities wanted respect too. Azazel said they must have sent spies to discover how to make swords and shields. This may have been true, but Tubal-Cain suspected Azazel had taught them. No matter how it came about, the results were the same. The cities of the land of Nod had all built up high walls around themselves to protect from the others and had armed themselves with swords and shields. There was constant war and bloodshed.

Tubal-Cain had been a simple maker of farm implements. Now, he was a supplier of death. He had lost too many of his neighbors to war and too much of his self-respect to greed and profits. He feared he would never go back to the innocence of his past.

Azazel and his wives he had chosen from the many cities and villages he visited had finally settled in a remote area northwest of Nod. He now had ten wives and twenty-two children. These children, however, were not ordinary in any way. They were, in all forms, strange and unique. Some were grotesquely shaped, while others were almost normal in appearance except for their size. Most were all at least nine cubits tall by the age of s▓▓▓▓▓▓▓▓made them two or three times the height of an ordinary man and five times the strength. They were also endowed with unique abilities.

The oldest, Syclah, had just one eye that was disoriented to the rest of his face. This made him a hideous sight to behold. Then, there was Harclah, the strong. He was one of the most powerful creatures alive. He once won a pulling match between himself and a behemoth, the most enormous creature that roamed the earth. There was Beodah, who could swim like a fish due to the strange webbing between his fingers and under his arms. His brother, Beodan, was the smallest of the giant children at the height of seven cubits. He was also the fastest and could leap great distances with ease. Sixteen others were terribly misshapen and slow of thought. These were sent to the far north and east for their ruthlessness and inability to control themselves. Then, there were the youngest two, Gardan and Skaldan, whose mother was an Enocian.

Gardan was the older of the two and was slightly shorter than Skaldan at the height of nine cubits. They were both mighty men; however, Skaldan was somewhat more assertive. He was less bright than Gardan, though. In fact, of all the freakish children, Gardan was the smartest. He was also the kindest and most conscientious of them all. He liked playing with some of the animals in the woods. Amazingly to his brothers, the animals, sensing his kindness, didn't seem to fear him.

One day, Syclah went into a rage and killed six of Azazel's wives, including Gardan's mother. Gardan was heartsick, but Azazel had just laughed about it and berated him for his emotional weakness. From that point on, this episode in his life fostered a hatred for his father and brothers that nearly turned his heart to stone. The fact that all the other children were hellishly cruel, not only to animals but to anyone they came in contact with, made Gardan very uncomfortable around them. He kept his distance as best he could. The only things Gardan didn't hate were the creatures that seemed to love him back. They were his only friends in the cruel world he was born into.

Azazel made the lives of the six brothers extremely difficult atop the secluded mountain upon which they remained hidden from the world. However, their father spoke frequently about a time in which he would release them to wreak havoc on the unsuspecting people in the lands below them as the other sixteen were now doing in the lands far to the east and north. Their father would conduct daily training exercises, pitting them against each other. He would then have the losers bound and beaten nearly to death to teach them the cruelty that the people of the world would show them if they allowed themselves to be harnessed by them.

Azazel was truly evil in the treatment of his sons and, for that matter, his wives. He would frequently beat his wives or, worse, have them tortured by their own children. He told them that they were now useless to him and only kept around for the sport of watching them beg for his mercy occasionally. Azazel truly enjoyed his complete control over this compound of hate and violence. When he lost control over the other sixteen children, he banished them from his sight. They were too unpredictable, and though he would not admit it, he feared they would retaliate against him for the cruelties he subjected them to. He thrived on control and would not lose it for any reason.

One day, Azazel called for a fight between Syclah and Gardan. Gardan hated fighting his brothers but also hated Syclah for what he did to his mother. Azazel despised the love that Gardan showed toward his mother and saw it as a threat to his supreme leadership. For this reason, Gardan suspected that what Syclah had done was more than just a loss of temper. He often wondered if Azazel had ordered the killing. His mother had spoken out about his treatment of her son the day before, only to be beaten severely. Gardan was held down and forced to watch while his brothers laughed and ridiculed him for his tears.

This day, however, Gardan had decided he had had enough of the cruelty of his father and brothers. When called to the fighting ring, he stood and said, "I no longer wish to do harm to my brothers! I will not fight them anymore." Walking toward his father, he continued, "You have pitted us against each other time and again; and for what purpose? It is only to satisfy your never-ending need for suffering and cruelty. No more, Father!"

Watching his father back away from him gave him a sense of control for the first time. Gardan could see the fear in his father's eyes, which gave him a satisfaction he had never felt before. He also had another feeling, an unwelcome feeling; pity. He couldn't believe he was actually feeling pity for this scared little man who had made his life a nightmare for all these years. He tried to push that pity aside as he drew nearer to Azazel. When his father ran out of room to retreat, Gardan clenched his fists and came within a few cubits of his poor excuse for a father. He had never felt a rage as was welling up inside him at this moment. He was clenching his teeth so hard that he could taste the blood running from his gums. He drew back to deal the blow that might finally put an end to this disgusting little man when he heard a whooshing sound from behind him. Suddenly, all went black.

Gardan regained an unsteady consciousness two days later in a place he did not recognize. He slid in and out, back and forth, from darkness to wakening, only to find himself in a different location every time. He was confused about how he was moving, not remembering any of it. He tried to get to his feet again but was met by the unnatural sound of grinding bones and piercing pain before the blackness enveloped him again. The next time he opened his eyes, he was in a cool, dark cavern. He could hear water running somewhere nearby but could not tell where. He thought he heard footsteps, then someone speaking, but once again, slipped into darkness.

Chapter 2

Year since creation: 682

WALKING THROUGH THE LUSHLY CARPETED VALLEY, ENOCH was in deep thought about the things he was just shown. He wasn't even sure how long he was gone. He had been taken from the earth to the stars, heaven, and back. He was shown things he was told to write down, but he needed to figure out how to describe them. He was only commanded to write them and trust the Creator to give him the words. In fact, the Lord had only just imparted the knowledge of those words to him. Now he must use those words to describe things that seemed wholly indescribable. How would he relate to his readers the beauty of even the floor of the Creator's throne room, much less the creatures that surrounded and worshiped Him? The fact was, he would have to teach this new knowledge of letters and writing to everyone before they could even read them. This seemed to him a daunting task for a simple farmer. He would obey, though. He would also count himself honored to be considered worthy of the Most High's mission.

"...then I was flying through the air inside some kind of house with crystal walls surrounded by a living fire that seemed to push it along," Enoch said while waving his arms in a self-mocking nature. He was, albeit comically, trying to imagine how his conversations would go when he told of his very recent adventure. "Then, I was in heaven looking through a transparent floor made of gold. Yes, I said transparent gold! Oh, and did I mention the angels with three sets of wings covered with eyes?"

There was also another message from the Lord he was given that gave him trouble. "What was that the angel told me about naming my son 'Methuselah?' What a strange name. He said to name him that because 'when he dies, then comes the destruction?' I'm not even married, yet the Lord is telling me about the death of my son. And what 'destruction' was the angel speaking of? How strange."

He shook his head and did the only thing he could do. He laughed at himself.

"If someone heard me talking to myself like this, they would think I had hit my head too hard," he thought. "No, I'll write it down and teach them to read so *everyone* can think I've hit my head too hard!"

At sixty years of age, Enoch wasn't generally the type of man to be overly emotional or given to whimsical fantasies. On the contrary, he was a sturdy, down-to-earth type who, in all things, faced life with the calm surety that came from his faith in the Lord. So, given what had just happened to him, it was quite out of character for him to be beside himself this way.

He was a man who loved to take frequent walks into the wilds of the Life-Giver's creation just for the sake of seeing, being awed by, and thanking Him for being placed into such a beautiful place as this earth. In fact, he loved to thank the Creator for *everything* he experienced. He felt that the Lord was always with him somehow. It was something he couldn't quite describe, but he had always felt the presence of the Lord with him. The Creator had never spoken directly to him, not verbally anyway. It had been hundreds of years since He had spoken directly to *anyone*, at least anyone he knew of.

Enoch's family elders would tell stories about those times at yearly celebratory harvest gatherings. He loved those stories. He liked to imagine what this world he loved to explore would have been like before it was spoiled by the terrible mistake that caused his greatest elder, Father Adam, to tremble in woeful remorse.

"The garden the Lord placed me and my lovely Eve into was simply perfect." Father Adam would say. "We were so blessed and blissfully unaware of what we had been given. The Creator provided for every want and desire of our hearts with a love and communion that can hardly be imagined by our now-corrupted and sinful minds. There were fruit trees and vegetables everywhere. The Lord planted them and tended them with His very thoughts. With a wave of His hand, a grove of figs would sprout. There were no thorns or thistles to choke them out as there are now. They were free to grow without restriction. The ground-springs would well up precisely where they were needed simply because the perfection of our world required it. All this, He did purely for our benefit; only because He loved us. He asked only one thing in return besides our love." Here, Father Adam broke down and sobbed in the heart-wrenching convulsions of a broken and repentant man.

He continued in broken words between emotional spasms, "We shouldn't have... disobeyed! He only... asked us not to... not to eat..." Then, with the gentle touch that could only come from his forever-faithful wife, he would melt into her understanding arms. Only she could console him this way. Only she truly understood the way he felt. Only she had been there with him on that terrible occasion. His tears were the tears of remorse, but the quiet tears shed by Mother Eve were the tears of guilt.

Mother Eve has carried the onus of her decision to eat the forbidden fruit, that terrible and delicious forbidden fruit, for six hundred and sixty years. She never spoke about it, but there was no way she could hide her shame when the subject of their former home came up. Out of respect for his elders, Enoch never broached this subject with Mother Eve or Father Adam. Still, what he knew of the Creator's love, He would not desire to have His "first-created" carry that load for their entire lives. However, Enoch felt this was something Father Adam and Mother Eve had to face alone.

As for Enoch, he was just content in his contemplations of that perfect world where he could take long walks and have in-depth conversations with his Lord right beside him, the God of all creation.

Preoccupied with thoughts of the visions he was shown, Enoch was nudged back into the here and now when he thought he heard a low, moaning sound. He stopped and quieted his breathing for a moment. There it was again. It was so soft and hushed that it surprised him he had heard it at all through the noise of his not-so-dainty footsteps. He listened again, trying to pinpoint a source for the faint sound. He heard it again, but it almost seemed to have an echoing quality to it. Enoch studied his surroundings to deduce the most likely location when, as he looked toward the closest valley wall, almost on cue, he heard it again even as he saw it. A cave opening was nearly hidden behind some boulders about thirty cubits from where he stood.

As he made his way toward the cave, he couldn't help but wonder how he had heard something so quiet from this great distance. His hearing was exceptional; however, as he drew nearer to the opening, the other-worldly noise didn't seem to be getting any louder. In fact, it seemed even quieter until he stood directly before the cave entrance. So much quieter that as he walked two steps into the earthly hollow and stopped to let his eyes adjust to the darkness, he thought he had looked in the wrong place after all.

Just as he turned to go back out, something caught his attention. He turned and walked a little further in. Enoch figured his eyes were still not adjusted well when he thought he saw a foot. What really surprised him and made him question his eyesight was the fact that this foot seemed to be three times the size of his own!

Enoch had seen big men before, men that were six cubits tall. Some had called them giants. There were also rumors of even larger men in some of the more remote villages of the lands far to the northeast. But Enoch had never heard of or seen anyone as big as the man that owned these feet.

He stood stark still, let his eyes adjust to the darkness a little better, and tried to think about his next step. "Was this huge being just taking a nap in the quiet, cool darkness of the cave? If so, how will he react if a comparatively puny man like *me* wakes him from his slumber?" Enoch thought to himself. "Then again, the noises he was making sounded more like the moans of a man in pain than a man having a dream. But I'm no expert on the sleeping habits of *giants*!"

That was when he was suddenly jolted from his moment of indecision. He watched with some apprehension as the huge man's feet began to move. He let out a loud wailing cry that instantly made Enoch's heart melt with compassion, as it would when he saw any of God's creatures hurt and in pain. At this moment, he also noticed the trail of blood left as this hulk of a man had dragged himself into this sanctuary of earth. It was a substantial amount in some places, while in others, it was lighter. Obviously, the heavier blood spots denoted where the man had stopped to rest.

That was when Enoch thought to himself, "Was he crawling into this rocky hole to get shade from the bright sun? Doing this in the pain this poor creature was in seems like too much work for a purpose that could have easily been accomplished with a large tree in the comfortable grasses throughout the valley. Could it be that this man was hiding from something? If so, *what*, or *who* would a man this large and powerful have been hiding from?" It was a frightening thought, but it didn't really matter in the end. This resident of creation required healing, and Enoch would help him. He just couldn't leave him there to suffer.

Now Enoch had a different problem altogether. Although he was a powerful man with the endurance of a horse, the job of moving this poor gigantic soul would be a monumental task. Enoch left the cave to weigh his options and stood under a sprawling tree several cubits away. He stood there looking out at this well-watered landscape to see what resources were available. There were some small branches from the many trees in the area. Many bulrushes down at the creek bed could be stripped and braided into a rope that could be used to fashion a makeshift liter to drag the large man out of the valley. However, this would require a few cutting tools and enormous strength to accomplish.

As he thought, he was startled by a man standing twenty cubits away, leaning against another tree with a beaming smile on his face. Though the man was in the shadow of the tree, there seemed to be a light that emanated from him. Enoch instantly knew what this glowing creature was. He had seen God's angels earlier in the day's adventures. He immediately fell to his face in awe of the brilliance of the angel's countenance. He asked God's forgiveness for his self-ramblings earlier.

"I beg the mercy of the Almighty and swear to Him that I will do all that He has told me to do! I will write down all that I was told and saw! I vow with all my soul that I will not question the Lord on what He has told me to do!" Enoch said as he lay trembling before this angel of the Lord.

"Stand up, son of Jared! It is forbidden for you to prostrate yourself before angels!" the holy being said to Enoch. "I am but a mere messenger of the One who deserves your praise. The Lord has sent me to tell you that He is pleased with you for heeding His Spirit and coming to the aid of this giant man for which He has chosen to show His mercy. The Creator has chosen you, His most faithful of servants, to be His instrument of grace to this poor lost soul," the angel said, motioning toward the cave.

"You are, however, not to tell *anyone* of this deed until a time in the future when the Lord makes it clear to do so. You are to nurse the man back to health where he now lays. This is the place the Lord has led him to for its proximity to the life-giving waters of this river and the fruits that grow along its banks. This valley also will protect him from the sight of those who would mean to do him harm until he is well again," said the angel.

The angel continued, "There will come a time when the Lord will bless you greatly for your deeds. He has great purpose for this mighty man entrusted to your care. This is what the Lord has told me to relate to you. Do all that you have been told with the kindness and mercy of the Spirit of the Creator."

With this, the angel vanished into the backdrop of the valley wall.

Enoch stood motionless for a while in reverence of what had just been told him. He then dropped to his knees and prayed for guidance and wisdom to accomplish the task entrusted to him. He stood to his feet again and walked over to fill his water gourd from the river. He brought it into the cave and gingerly poured some of the water into the mouth of this giant to be used by God. Leaving the gourd next to the giant man, he departed the cave.

"I will be back tomorrow with bandages and salves to treat your wounds," he said to the sleeping hulk. With that, he turned to make the trek back to his farm. All the way home, he excitedly thought of how much his life had changed in a single day. This had been the most eventful day of his sixty years of life, and he suspected that his life would never be the same.

Chapter 3

Year since creation: 703

THE MIDDAY SUN SHONE BRIGHTLY OVER THE SPRAWLING
farmland nestled amid a magnificent valley. The pure
cold springs that fed the valley poured out of the mountains at
the north end and meandered through the valley floor below,
breaking apart here and there, dispensing its life-giving refresh-
ments almost equally to every part of this rich and fertile terrain. On the east side of the valley ran the main body of water
that fed the many small streams and tributaries. This river was
teeming with creatures of all sorts. It was surrounded by birds
and flying things ranging from hummingbirds the size of a man's
thumbnail to airborne serpents the size of a small house. All
fed on the lush grasses and nectars of the natural gardens that
carpeted the riversides.

While Enoch walked down into this valley he called home, the
first thing that invaded his senses, besides the uncanny beauty of
the scenery, was the fragrant odor of a thousand different types
of flowering plants and fruits that spread their way across the
ideally situated and picturesque countryside. The white, yellow,
blue, orange, red, and purple orchids of all types and the deep
green and browns of the eighty-cubit-tall cypress trees that grew

in the marshier areas of the river's edge always made Enoch pause and wonder if he had rediscovered the lost Eden of Father Adam.

The farmland that dominated the valley's center was precisely placed along and between the many streams and brooks that weaved their way throughout the flatlands. The rows of corn and wheat followed perfectly with the shapes dictated by the swaying of the waterways. In the center of the farmland was an equally ideally placed farmhouse with a whisp of smoke rising from the chimney stack and filling the air with the sweet aroma of baking honey bread and stew.

Enoch was, as usual, deep in thought as he descended the path and over the tiny bridges that led to his home. He was returning from one of his famous "walks" where he could be gone for days, getting lost in the natural beauty of his surroundings. His wife, Ednah, used to get upset with him about his wanderings. However, over the past twenty years, she had learned to accept that it was his way and that she could do nothing to change him. Besides, she didn't want to change him. He was, at least as far as she was concerned, the most loving and attentive husband she could ever want.

Enoch made his way over the final bridge on the path to the house. He reached down and picked one of Ednah's favorite lilies from the flower garden he had planted for her after their first child, Methuselah, was born. He thought of how much his life had changed over the last twenty-one years.

Now, at eighty-one, he was still in the prime of his relative youth. Enoch's skin was bronzed from his many hours in the sun, and at a little over four cubits, he was a bit taller than average. He wasn't overly muscular but was very strong and sinewy due to the farming he had done from his youth. His hair was a darkish auburn, without a hint of the grey that had, of late, invaded his father's head, and flowed easily over his shoulders with a slight natural curl. His eyes were a deep, thoughtful blue.

Enoch felt, however, that he had led a pretty full life for a man his age. He had gotten closer to his God than he had ever thought possible. The Lord would even occasionally join him in his walks just for the "pleasure of his company," as the Lord would put it. Enoch would ask the Lord's advice on things ranging from child care to dealing with the mood swings of a wife with an oft-wandering husband. The Creator would also ask Enoch how he felt about things ranging from the weather to the cultural happenings in the cities around this area of the world. Enoch knew that the Lord was already aware of how he felt about these things but was always in awe of how very personable the Lord could be.

Enoch quietly walked onto the house's front porch and stealthily opened the front door. He could hear Ednah singing to their daughter, Mirah, in the kitchen area while she cleaned her baking pots in the wash-tub he had built for her. Three-year-old Mirah noticed him first as Enoch eased his way into the kitchen. He quickly put his hand over his mouth, looking at the bright-eyed little girl with a playful expression on his face. She aped his movements and followed his cues so as not to make his presence known to her still-unaware mother. Enoch slowly reached out his hand with the lily and lightly brushed Ednah's right ear with its soft petals. She absentmindedly threw her hand up to shoo away the gnat she thought was buzzing her ear. Again, Enoch ever so lightly caressed her ear with the lily. This time she turned her head slightly and wafted her hand at the bothersome gnat, but she caught sight of something out of the corner of her eye.

With a startled shriek, she whirled around and dumped an entire baking pot full of soapy water onto the head of her equally-startled husband. They stood there with mouths agape and stared at each other for just a moment. Mirah was the first to make a sound as she squealed with delight over the sight of her father, with suds forming a comical mound on the top of his head and face dripping wet. Then Ednah nearly dropped the pot as she quickly tried to put it back in the wash-tub while simultaneously hugging her husband. For a few moments, they all enjoyed the rich laughter of a happy family who was together again.

Ednah was a beautiful young woman of seventy years who still had the youthful figure and cuteness of a teenager. She had an olive complexion that contrasted nicely with her sandy blonde hair and delicate features with bright green eyes that Enoch had always found striking. She also carried herself with a dignified, almost royal grace that belied her simple life on the farm.

Once she composed herself again, she smiled a mischievous little smile at him, saying, "You better stop sneaking up on me that way, or you'll end up wearing that pot on your head! What if that was a boiling pot of stew?"

Reaching out with the now-drooping lily, he said, "Then, I suppose I would deserve it just as much as you deserve this token of my love, my dearest Ednah."

"Now look what you went and made me do!" She took the lily and vainly tried to stand it upright again, "Your sneaking up on me like that is going to be the death of me. I'd like you to know that you've taught your son to do that too. Between the two of you, I'm going to be a bundle of nerves."

"Where is that son of mine anyway?" asked Enoch, looking through the window opening and scanning side to side, searching the farm for any sign of his sixteen-year-old son.

"He and Jubal said they were going down to the swamp to find something to do," answered Ednah as she went back to her pot washing.

Enoch shook his head and muttered to himself, "That boy better not be toying with that poor thing again."

The two boys trudged through the muddy marshland to the south of the farm, heading toward what they hoped would be an adventure. Methuselah spoke excitedly about the plan, "We'll have to be very quiet if we hope to get close enough to put the bridle on him. Now, once I get it on him, I need you to take the long end and wrap it a few times around a tree trunk so he won't be able to start running. Once he calms down a bit, you can give him more rope."

"*If* he calms down, you mean," said Jubal, a bit warier of his cousin's so-called plan. "What makes you think that it's going to just calm down at all? Maybe we should find something else to do this afternoon before getting ourselves hurt. Besides, your father has warned us to stay away from the leviathan down here."

Jubal was a bright and cautious boy most of the time. But, when it came to Methuselah, Jubal seemed to have a weakness for his sheer enthusiasm and confidence.

Jubal was Methuselah's cousin from the next valley over to the west. His dirty blonde hair and square jaw made him a very handsome young man at the height of four cubits. He had deep brown eyes and was powerfully built due to his farm work since the age of three. Now sixteen, he was the most sought-after boy in the valleys, save one; Methuselah.

Though Jubal had rugged good looks, he was quiet and shy. On the other hand, Methuselah had more refined looks and a silvery-smooth tongue to match. He was slightly taller than Jubal, with raven-colored hair that had just a bit of waviness. With his bright aqua-blue eyes and the ability to eloquently phrase things in such a way that made him seem wise beyond his years, the girls would just melt before him.

But Methuselah had his sights set on just one girl; Tamari. Since he was eight years old, he knew that she and she alone was the girl for him. Jubal had, for nearly just as long, liked her sister Julis. This fact had always seemed to the two boys to be a sign from the Almighty that life was destined to go in the natural progression laid out before them. As far as they were concerned, nothing would or could change that fact. This unshakable idealism was a good quality in the two boys; however, it could also get them into trouble. The latter seemed to be the case today.

"Just because Father has never *seen* a tamed leviathan doesn't mean that one cannot be tamed," Methuselah retorted. "Think about it Jubal. What do you suppose Tamari and Julis will think of us once we get our leviathan trained enough to ride him to the festival in Urna next month?"

"They'll think we're crazy for bringing such a dangerous beast into the public and never want to see us again! What do you suppose the people of Urna will think if that thing starts spewing fire everywhere?" asked Jubal. "Look, I know you're not going to change your mind about doing this, but I want to let it be known, I don't think this is a good idea. I need you to promise me that *if* you live through this, you'll tell your father that I tried to talk you out of it."

"But we have thought this through..." said Methuselah before Jubal interrupted.

"Just promise me," he said, throwing his hand up. "I'm not saying I'm not going to help you. I just don't want to have to pull the whole farm full of weeds again like I did before when you talked me into painting my father's ox red so that it was easier for my mother to see where father was in the field."

"I'll tell him. I'll tell him," said Methuselah. "Now, let's go."

The boys started into the swamp, being as quiet as they could. They went about thirty cubits in when Methuselah raised his hand and pointed to a spot in front of him to signal the location of their prey. Jubal eased over to him to get a closer look at what they were about to get themselves into. There, sleeping on the edge of the water, was a leviathan.

The creature was, to say the least, intimidating. This massive lizard was every bit of twenty-five cubits long and three cubits high with rock-hard scales from the tip of its snout to the spiked end of its tail. Its mouth was open just far enough to see its jagged teeth between its slimy green lips. Each of its teeth was about a third of a cubit long and was stained greenish-yellow from the fodder it chewed for food. Though the boys did not fear it wanting to eat them, the sheer power this beast possessed could easily break them in half. As if these things weren't frightening enough, there was also the flame-shooting problem. When angry, it had the ability to spew a flame up to fifteen cubits away, and do it with some degree of accuracy. This was not a creature to be taken lightly.

Methuselah handed Jubal the straight end of the rope. At the same time, he held the end where he had fashioned a sizeable makeshift bridle to throw over the head of this sleeping giant. Attached to the bridle was another shorter piece of rope that was tied around Methuselah's waist. This was his bright idea, which was supposed to keep him from falling off before he could "break the creature's will enough to control it."

Tiptoeing around to get himself in a better position to throw the bridle over the creature's head, he motioned for Jubal to wrap the rope around a small tree growing out of the mud a few cubits away. Methuselah was ready. He slowly swung the bridle back and forth a few times to get the feel of it and aim at his target, then let it go. It landed perfectly in place. Methuselah smiled big at Jubal to show his pride at a job well done and picked up his foot to swing himself onto the back of his new toy. As he picked his foot out of the mud, it made a loud sucking sound as the thick mud released his foot. He stopped mid-action and looked at Jubal with wide eyes as he saw the giant lizard's large eyes slowly open up.

Suddenly, the creature realized it was not alone and sprang from its resting spot, darting forward, taking Methuselah with it, who was now attached by the waist to the bridle. The monster bounded through the underbrush before circling back around because of being pulled by the other end of the rope wrapped around the tree near where Jubal stood in wide-eyed terror. As the creature came back past Jubal, he held the rope tight. He needed to control the angry lizard long enough for Methuselah to free himself at the other end. The creature passed him, and he watched as the rope reached its limit. He was ready to see the beast come to a sudden halt at the end of its tether. Then, to his amazement, he looked down at empty hands. The mighty beast had, in an instant, pulled the tree right up out of the muddy ground and pulled the rope out of his now burning hands. He looked up to see the tree, the creature, and his best friend, disappear into the deeper parts of the swamp that led out to the river. He saw them turn upstream toward the north and the farm. Jubal thought, "What will become of Methuselah, and what will I tell his father?"

Enoch was walking down the path toward the swamps to see what the boys were up to. Methuselah had always been an adventurous spirit, but Enoch couldn't help but be concerned for his safety this time more than any other to this point. The Lord had told him to pray immediately after finding out where they had gone. As he walked down the path and prayed, he heard a shrieking scream in the distance. He then heard the splashing of an enormous creature, and it seemed to be getting closer. He looked toward the river and saw a great wake in the waters. Breaking the surface was the leviathan he had warned his son about, driving out of the water and onto the river bank with Methuselah hanging on for dear life. He was being thrown around from side to side like a little girl's doll while screaming for help.

Enoch had to act quickly. He stepped forward and did the only thing he knew to do with a problem this big. He raised his hands and prayed for the words to speak to this angry creature that would calm him and spare his son.

"Leviathan, halt!" he yelled.

Instantly, the hulking giant came to a sudden stop, causing Methuselah to come to rest, hanging by the waist alongside. His father came to him and pulled the rope at the knot around his waist, and Methuselah flopped to the ground, limp and exhausted. After removing the bridle from the annoyed leviathan, Enoch lovingly reached down and picked Methuselah up to his feet, "Come on, son. You've had enough fun for one day." Then, turning to the creature who looked equally exhausted, he said, "Go back to your home. You won't be bothered anymore today."

The great lizard turned calmly and walked back to the river, where it was slowly enveloped by the water and gone with hardly a ripple.

Jubal ran into the yard as Enoch and Methuselah were about to enter the house. Jubal, panting after the long run, was trying to catch his breath so he could tell Enoch something, but Enoch already knew how his son was when he got an idea into his head.

"It's alright, Jubal," he said, holding his free hand up open-palmed. "I don't hold you responsible. I know my son well."

With that, Jubal turned to go home. He wasn't sure how Methuselah's father was able to get the creature to stop and let him go, but he was truly glad. He prayed his thanksgivings all the way home.

Chapter 4

METHUSELAH AWOKE AT MIDDAY FROM A HEAVY SLEEP. HE usually wouldn't sleep this long, but he *usually* didn't go leviathan-riding either. As he stirred, he was immediately met with the consequences of the previous day's adventures. His muscles were on fire, his hands were nearly skinned, and he had a headache; all this was his reward for a very dumb decision.

"Oh…Oh my…my head…oooh…" he grumbled as he tried to rise up on his elbow. He slowly pulled off the blanket and realized that even the muscles in his fingers hurt, along with every other muscle he attempted to move.

"How are we feeling this morning?" asked his mother as she approached his slightly open door. "A little sore, I'd guess? Well, I *hope* so!" now with her hands on her hips in that motherly way. "Do you know how close you came to getting yourself killed yesterday!?" she said, even as she came over and hugged him.

At this, he winced in pain, "Mother, that hurts! Ouch, ouch."

"That's your own fault. This wouldn't have happened at all if you had listened to your father in the first place. What would have happened if he wasn't there to stop that creature from dragging you off to who *knows* where?" she said with a tear in her eye. "Don't ever try anything like that again. Do you hear me?" as she hugged him again, once more making Methuselah wince in pain.

"This wasn't some silly way of trying to impress Tamari, was it?" she asked with her hands back on her hips. "If she's half the girl I think she is, she would think it was just as stupid as I do. I'm guessing she would probably think twice before getting too involved with a boy who makes such dumb decisions as the one you made yesterday."

"Alright, Mother, alright," Methuselah said with his hands up in a surrendering gesture. "I get it. I promise not to try and ride them anymore. Trust me, Mother. I know now how dumb it was," he said as he rubbed his neck, making a face that matched his pain.

"So, are you hungry? I picked you some berries and melon this morning," she said as she left the room and returned to the kitchen area.

"I thought you were mad at me?" he said as he stood, stretched, and walked out of his room. His mother just turned and gave him a whimsical smile. She knew that Methuselah loved melon and berries for breakfast. In her own way, she was trying to make up for the tongue-lashing she had just given him. Besides, to Enoch's dismay, she loved to spoil this son of hers.

Over his breakfast, which he was sharing with his three-year-old little sister, Mirah, as she ran around the room flapping her arms like a bird and singing to herself, he and his mother discussed the things happening in and around their lives.

"So, how are you and Tamari getting on these days?" asked Ednah. She would often ask him about her just to see him light up. In many ways, he was like his father. Enoch still lit up that way for her, and it made her happy that her son felt that same kind of love for Tamari. She knew long ago that this was the girl for him, and that was fine with her. She had grown to love Tamari like a daughter already. Tamari had a sweet spirit about her and an easy smile that made her son melt. She was also a very bright girl with a sharp wit and, with it, seemed to be easily capable of putting Methuselah in his place when he needed it. However, she was able to do it with a grace that would allow her son to keep his dignity. Ednah hadn't told her or Methuselah about how strongly she felt. Still, she had already resigned herself to the fact that Tamari would be the ideal daughter-in-law.

"We're fine, Mother," he grunted as he shifted in his seat, trying vainly to find a spot on his bottom that wasn't bruised.

"When are you supposed to see her again? I need her to take this honeybread to her mother." Tamari's mother hadn't asked for the bread, but Ednah wanted to try and reach out to her. She had tried to speak to her a few times before, but she had seemed standoffish and hard to talk to. There weren't many people that Ednah didn't like, but this woman seemed to have a knack for rubbing her the wrong way. There was something about Tamari's mother that made Ednah feel uneasy. Still, she was bound and determined to get this woman to like her. So be it if it took sending her some of her famous honeybread.

"I'm going to see her this afternoon. She wanted us to have a picnic at the pond up in the valley pass. I was going to ask you if you had some extra bread made," Methuselah said. He smiled that begging smile that he knew she couldn't resist.

"Do you think I have nothing to do but bake you bread all day?" she asked playfully, even as she pulled more out of the box on the counter.

"Thank you, Mother. I love you," he said as he kissed her cheek and limped toward the door. "I'm going to talk to Father. I might as well get it over with. Is he still angry with me?"

"Yes, but not because of what you did so much as the fact that he had already warned you about it. Just get ready for a lecture," Ednah replied.

He just nodded and headed out the door. Methuselah had been on the receiving end of his father's lectures before. It wasn't pleasant, but it could be worse. He supposed he could still be getting dragged all across creation by that giant lizard. In that case, he was glad to get that lecture.

He was greeted outside by a beautiful day. The cool mists were wafting through the valley, bringing moisture to the emerald crops. He couldn't see his father immediately and decided to get on top of a rock in one of the four little flower gardens his father had planted for his mother out in front of the house. As he scanned the scenery about him, he found his father in a chair near the stream that ran closest to the house. This was one of his father's favorite spots to sit and watch the fledgling little fish that gathered in the shallow nursery that had formed in the inside corner of the stream. He so enjoyed seeing them flit and play, and he was even known to talk to them occasionally like a proud father. A large cedar tree there provided good shade during the hottest part of the day. It aided in keeping the small pool at a relatively moderate temperature. It made for a stunningly beautiful spot where one could sit, relax, contemplate, and pray. Praying was what Enoch was doing now.

Methuselah walked over but kept his distance so as not to interrupt him. He liked to hear his father pray. It had always impressed him how his father would speak to the Lord as if He were right there next to him. It also impressed him how his father always thanked the Creator for everything, even the things that were not so nice to go through. One year, a fire had started in his storehouse, and took the season's whole crop with it. His father dropped to his knees when the fire was finally put out. Instead of crying or complaining, he started singing praises to the Lord for the opportunity to see the Creator's goodness and faithfulness to those who were faithful to Him.

Methuselah didn't quite understand what goodness or faithfulness his father was referring to until the next afternoon when his family elders, Kenan, Mahalalel, and Jared, came to the house. Each carried a full third of the stores required for him and his family to get through the next growing season. They all said that they were told in a dream that they were to do this. They also noted that their harvests were especially large that year and now understood why. This, and many other happenings, was why Methuselah would keep his father's faith and honor the Creator daily.

Having finished with his prayers, Enoch looked up at the stream and, sensing his presence, asked Methuselah to join him.

"Son, why do you worry your mother so?" he asked with a heavy sigh. "You make her a very nervous woman when you do these things."

"I'm sorry Father. I know. She just scolded me for it. I promised her I wouldn't try to ride the leviathan again," he said with his head down in shame for worrying her and disappointing his father.

"I suppose she gave you this scolding just before feeding you your favorite breakfast of fresh berries and melon?" he asked.

Methuselah paused for an awkward moment before answering, "Yes, Father."

"I saw her picking them this morning and figured just as much. The way she spoils you is not good for you, but there is nothing I will ever be able to do about that. After all, she spoils me the same way and I honestly don't know if I would want to change that either," he said with a mischievous smile. "Sit next to me son and enjoy watching the fish with me. I need to talk with you about something."

Still feeling the soreness in his joints, Methuselah slowly sat on the soft grass next to his father's chair.

"Methuselah, do you think that I could make one of these fish perform a task for me?" Enoch asked.

Methuselah pursed his lips and looked sideways at his father, "No, I don't think so. They aren't like that. They just do... what fish do."

Enoch nodded and gave an approving look to his son, "You are right, Son. These fish weren't meant to serve man in the way that the oxen or sheep or horses are. They were placed here for our enjoyment, but not for our domination." He paused to let that sink in. "In the same way, the leviathan are a lot like these fish. They are meant for a different purpose. They are meant to be free to do what leviathan do. Do you understand what I am saying?"

"I think so, Father. I guess I never thought about it that way," he said with a contemplative look on his face.

"Good," Enoch said as he slapped his knees and smiled at his son. "How is that pretty girl of yours?"

"Pretty as ever, Father. I'm going to meet her at the pond up in the pass today. We're supposed to have a picnic."

"Good," said Enoch, "give her my regards. I really like that girl. She will make an excellent daughter-in-law someday."

Methuselah said nothing, but the red face told Enoch that he had done with that comment what it was meant to do. Enoch chuckled.

With some difficulty and rubbing his achy legs, Methuselah got up and started to walk back toward the house. He stopped and turned back to his father with a perplexed look.

"Father, you said that I made Mother nervous when I did things like I did yesterday. Weren't you also worried about me?" he asked.

Enoch turned back to the stream and momentarily thought about that question before answering, "I am always concerned for you, Son. However, the Lord has a special destiny for you to fulfill. Being dragged across the face of the earth by an angry beast like that is *not* your destiny."

This made Methuselah pause with interest, "What destiny is that, Father?"

Enoch smiled and laughed, "You will have to try and stay out of trouble long enough to find out. The Lord will reveal that to you in time."

Methuselah just shook his head and walked away with a slight limp. Enoch inwardly thought about what he could not tell his son about the future and muttered under his breath, "In time, my son; just how much time, you have no idea."

Chapter 5

METHUSELAH WAS ON HIS WAY TO MEET WITH TAMARI WITH the picnic basket in his still-sore hand. He couldn't wait to see her, and it was evident by the jovial spring in his step and the tune he was whistling despite his aching muscles and bruises. He was still some distance away and crossing the last stream before beginning his ascent to the low pass.

He couldn't keep his mind on anything other than the bright smile he was on his way to behold. Tamari was a very well-put-together girl with naturally curly strawberry-blonde hair and large green eyes. She has a playful laugh that somehow made Methuselah's heart skip a beat. Though she wasn't perfect, he couldn't think of what any of those imperfections might be. She was everything to him, and he wanted her to know it. Though he was still very young, this was the day he would make his intentions known. He wanted to promise himself to her in marriage and hoped desperately that she would accept. However, he couldn't imagine her refusing. She was his, and, as far as he was concerned, they both knew it.

He was just coming over the final rise and craned his neck to see if she was already there. Then he saw her. Sitting amid a patch of wildflowers along the pond's edge, she sang to herself. She had a beautiful voice with a sweet melodic quality. He slowed his walking so as not to make his presence known to her just yet. He finally stopped and listened for a few moments before moving closer.

"How is my little songbird today?" Then, feigning a surprised look, "Oh, I thought that *was* a songbird singing up here," he said with a beaming smile. "Just as well; I would hate for you to fly away."

"You are very kind my dear, but do you really think all that sweet talk is going to get you any points with me?" said Tamari as she excitedly got up and skipped toward him.

"Yes, I do. At least I hope so," he responded with an inquiring smile.

She took a deep breath and smiled back at him before embracing him. Then, in a quiet, sweet voice that could melt the hardest heart, she answered, "I'm afraid you know me too well."

While in the tight squeeze of her embrace, she noted a slight painful moan from him and pushed him back so she could see the grimace on his face.

"Are you alright? What's the matter?" she asked.

Methuselah evasively answered her, "I'm alright. I just got a little bruised up yesterday fooling around with Jubal. Don't worry yourself about it. I'm just a little sore. It will pass."

She knew how adventurous Methuselah could be and was pretty sure she probably wouldn't want to know any more than that. This young man of hers was nearly fearless, and for no tangible reason, it excited her. She sometimes worried about *how* adventurous he could be, but that was also part of what made him so irresistible.

"Well, are you ready to eat?" he asked her as he opened the basket and began setting out the food on the blanket she had already spread out in anticipation of their picnic.

"Yes," she said. "It has been a long time since breakfast and I could probably eat the whole basket myself."

They spent the hours playfully talking and eating, occasionally feeding each other the way young lovers do. It was a fantastic afternoon, and Methuselah anticipated that the question he wanted to ask her would be received quite well.

"Oh, I didn't realize how late it was getting," said Tamari when she noticed how low the sun was getting in the sky. "Father will be upset with me if it gets too dark before I get home."

Methuselah jumped up to help gather the scraps of food and the blanket, "Can I walk with you to the bottom of the pass? I've got something to ask you along the way."

"Why, I would be honored," she said with a slight bow of the head.

As they turned to start their walk, they noticed three young men coming from the path along the ridge. Almost immediately, Methuselah recognized the boys.

"Oh no," he said under his breath. "Just politely nod to them. We don't want any trouble today. It has been such a nice day and I don't want anything to spoil it."

Rimlah and his friends were approaching them and giggling to each other. Methuselah didn't really hate anyone, but this boy and his hangers-on were very dislikable. Rimlah's father was one of Urna's political leaders and was very wealthy. As a result, Rimlah thought he was above anyone that didn't measure up to his station in life. However, he had always taken a keen liking to Tamari. This was at the root of the ongoing issues between Methuselah and his archenemy, Rimlah. But today was not the day for fighting.

"Look, it's the farmer boy and your girl," said Ortha, Rimlah's friend to his left.

"What are we going to have to do to get this fool to leave her alone, Rimlah?" asked the other one, Keman.

"Look fellows, I'm just trying to get her home before she gets into trouble for being too late," said Methuselah, trying to use the fact that Rimlah, for all his faults, really did like Tamari and, hopefully, wouldn't want to see her get in any serious trouble on his account.

Tamari chimed in, "Please, Rimlah, he's telling you the truth. I really need to get on home."

"I've got an idea," responded Rimlah. "Why don't you send this poor boy on his way and *we* can make sure you get home safely. Besides, my sweet, you need to spend some time with a *real* man before you start thinking *this* is what a man is supposed to be," he said, motioning toward Methuselah.

Methuselah could feel the anger rising in his throat and the heat rising in his face. "Not now," he told himself calmly, "just laugh it off and try to defuse this situation." He put on his most friendly smile, "Alright, gentlemen, you've had your fun. We're going to go now before the lady gets in any trouble. So, if you'll excuse us." He grabbed Tamari by the hand and tried to maneuver around the human roadblocks on the path.

Rimlah seemed to relent and moved back to let them pass, but Ortha, who wasn't known for being too bright, missed the cue and grabbed the basket out of Methuselah's hand. He tossed it to Keman when Methuselah reached to take it back. Keman opened it, grabbed the two loaves of bread for Tamari's mother, and threw them into the pond.

Sensing that Methuselah had about all he would take, she squeezed his hand and said, "It's alright, sweetheart. It's only bread. Let's just go."

He relented, and with all the civility he could muster, he started walking again. At this point, the picnic basket hit him in the back of the head and then deflected and hit Tamari. That was all he could take. He could not and would not hold back any longer. He was about the same height as these three boys but was in much better shape and incredibly strong due to years of hard farm work. These rich boys were soft, pampered, and slow.

He turned and exploded in a flash onto Ortha, who was the closest to him. In a moment, he had punched him in the face, the gut, and the face again before tossing him aside like a chair in his way. Then he was on the move toward a surprised Keman. Before he could cover his face, Methuselah had grabbed Keman by the hair and pulled his face down into his waiting kneecap. Two down, and he was on his way toward Rimlah, who stood there with his mouth agape.

Tamari shouted, "Stop Methuselah! Stop!"

By this time, Rimlah was backing up as fast as he could to escape the crazed young man before him. He finally stopped when he realized that he was standing up to his knees in the pond. At this point, Methuselah stopped his advance, looked down at the tiny little man in the water, and slowly allowed his temper to ebb. In fact, the longer he looked at him standing there like a scared little wet rat, the more he allowed a mocking smile to don his face. He turned to look at Tamari, who also started to smile.

He turned back to Rimlah and said, "Now, it is you who will go home. If you ever bother Tamari or me again, you will get the same treatment as your two pathetic friends over there. Do we have an understanding?"

Rimlah didn't know what to say. He was embarrassed at the fact that he was hiding in the safety of the pond, which, in turn, made him angry. But he also knew better than to try and match skills with the young man before him. He had but one choice at this point.

He just nodded his agreement and walked a circular route out of the pond and around Methuselah. His woozy friends were beginning to come around now and trying to stand to their feet.

"I'll get you for this!" spouted Ortha as he nursed his aching nose.

"Quiet, you useless idiot!" said Rimlah angrily. "You two are completely useless!" And, they were off, back across the ridge toward the city of Urna.

"Thank you, Methuselah. I'm sorry for all of this. I don't know what I did to make him think I would ever be interested in him. Why will he not take a hint?" said Tamari.

"Just a bit dense, I suppose," said Methuselah.

"I guess so," said Tamari. "Oh, I've got to go now! It's almost dark and my father is going to be so angry. I love you, Methuselah. I'll see you later."

With that, she ran down the path as fast as she could. Methuselah stood and watched her disappear in the waning light before he turned to head in the opposite direction. He couldn't help but feel a bit of satisfaction in putting that set of oafs in their place. They had it coming for a long time. However, somehow, he had the feeling that this was not over. Spoiled little rich boys didn't take too well to embarrassing themselves in front of their underlings like that.

There was also the disappointment that he didn't have the chance to ask the one thing he wanted to ask today. No harm; he would get another chance in a few days. He was sure of it. As he walked home, he replayed her last words to him over and over in his mind, "I love you, Methuselah." Nothing he had ever heard sounded as sweet.

Chapter 6

As Tamari ran into the yard amidst her family farm, there was just enough light to see her father, Jaylon, standing on the porch with his arms folded. He was not happy. On more than one occasion, he had expressed concern for his daughter seeing this boy from that strange family in the next valley. He had no specific dealings with Enoch or his family that made him dislike them. However, the strange visions, or dreams, or *whatever* he called them, were very disturbing to many of the families in the valleys, and for that matter, to the people in Urna.

Many years ago, Enoch had told everyone that the Lord had charged him with the task of teaching all His children a system of letters and writing so that they could read the messages given to them through these writings. It was odd to most people, but Enoch was among the most respected and revered men around. He was always known to do what was right and fair in all his ways.

He taught the family elders in each valley and town so that they, in turn, would teach the rest of the family. He had also taught his elder, Seth, the king of the earth, who appointed scribes to keep Enoch's writings in the royal chambers of knowledge. In this way, they could be passed down to every generation.

Since then, this writing system has become a valuable part of their society and has aided in all manner of business, especially in the cities. Still, there was some resentment to Enoch's insistence that he was the conduit of the Creator's knowledge and revelations to the rest of the people. He was a simple farmer. So, the city leaders, and in turn, the people who ran after the power these men could give them, were threatened by the unwavering respect given to Enoch's words.

Jaylon had also been a simple farmer until a few years ago when he had found that the caves on a portion of his farm were loaded with some of the most spectacular emeralds anyone had ever seen. He saw this as his way out of the hard work of a farmer and into the world of the prosperous and important. He quickly left behind the plowing for the mining business. He still grew what his family needed, but he now hired others to do the hard work. He and his wife, Naamah, had come to immensely enjoy the respect and admiration that their newly acquired wealth afforded them. They had elevated themselves to a higher station in life. He couldn't stand the thought of his daughter marrying this mere farm boy with the strange family line. Yes, his family elder was the king, but Enoch and his family didn't seem to have what he saw as the good sense to act like it.

Now, seeing the distress on her father's face, Tamari tried to head off his anger, "Father, I'm sorry that it got so dark before I could…"

Jaylon cut her off, not wanting to hear her excuses, "You were with Methuselah, weren't you? I do not want to hear it! I have told you about that boy. Have I not told you about that boy?"

"But Father, it wasn't his fault. I swear, it…." was all she could get out of her mouth.

"Does that stupid boy even *care* that you will get in trouble for being so late?" he said, red-faced and indignant. "Does he even regard you with enough honors to keep you from punishment? I do not want you to see him anymore. You are too good for that boy, and I'll not have him treating you this way again!"

"But Father, you don't understand. I would have been home well before now if it weren't for…" she sputtered as tears began to well up in her eyes.

"I said I do not want to hear it. That is final! Now go inside before your mother starts crying again from the worry that boy has caused this family." he said, pointing to the house.

Tamari could no longer form words and was on the verge of wailing aloud as she rushed past her father and through the door.

She had tried everything she knew to get her parents to like Methuselah. She insisted on inviting his family over for dinner, only to have them be somewhat polite when they were there and then talked down about as backward and stupid when they left. All they would ever say was, "You can do so much better than that farm boy." Or, they would say, "There are some very nice boys in the city if you would only give them a chance." This only meant that the boys they had in mind were wealthy and well-connected. She knew her parents only too well. She hated feeling this way but couldn't get away from the fact that they were only using her to get to the next level of stature in the eyes of the city leaders.

As she ran inside, she went directly to her bedroom. Her mother tried to speak to her but was quickly brushed aside and left standing in the ornately decorated receiving room of the house. Judging the situation, Naamah decided to let her be for now. She would calm down eventually.

Jaylon came through the door, breathing heavily after the altercation. He hated yelling at his daughter this way. It frustrated him that she would not see his reasoning in these matters. There was a time when he could not imagine such a verbal battle with Tamari, but those times seemed long gone. Over the last few years, this type of thing has become increasingly common.

"What are we to do about this?" he asked his wife. "She just doesn't seem to see that we only want the best for her. If she stays with that boy, she will be relegated to the menial life of a farmer's wife. Doesn't *she* want better for *herself*? I just do not understand what she sees in that boy. Is there something more to him than I can see?"

Naamah put her hand on his tense shoulder and said softly, to calm him, "She says that he treats her with love and tenderness. That is good, but she is young and idealistic. She doesn't yet understand that there is much more to life than that." She paused momentarily, "You know, I think if she sees what life might be like for her if she were to marry a boy of higher quality, she would have the good sense to leave Methuselah alone to find himself some grubby little farm girl."

Jaylon looked at her as a thought crossed his mind, "What if I invited Leader Bertlaw and his wife and son here for lunch? He has said on more than one occasion that he thought Tamari was a very suitable match for his son."

"Leader Bertlaw," she said with a twinkle in her eye. "I think that is a wonderful idea. What is his son like? I don't believe I have ever met him."

"I haven't met him either, but we know he comes from a good family. His father is one of the wealthiest men in Urna. I will set it up for a few days from now. This will be ideal. However, I still do not know if it will be enough to turn the head of our daughter away from Methuselah. She has cared for him for so long," said Jaylon.

Naamah thought about that for a moment before a mischievous smile came across her face, "I believe I have an idea that will work to put things into a proper light for her. You just set up the luncheon, and I will handle everything else."

It was completely dark by the time Methuselah arrived at his house. His mother was sitting out on the porch and had her arms folded with a knowing smile on her face. "Methuselah, please tell me that you walked her all the way home, and that's why you're so late getting home. You know, her father isn't going to like it very much that you keep her out this long."

"Don't worry, Mother, it wasn't my fault she was late," he answered. "Besides, I think she got home before dark."

She looked at him with a quizzical eye, "Well, what was it then?"

"It's a long story, Mother," he said.

"Well, perhaps you should start telling it then," replied his father, who had walked up behind him, startling him with his deep, loud voice. Enoch loved to do that to him and had a grin on his face to prove it.

The family walked into the house and sat around the table while Methuselah related the entire story of what had happened at the pond. Enoch listened thoughtfully as his son told his tale, complete with reenactments and dramatic inflections. His parents tried not to laugh at their son, but they both found it quite comical.

When all was told, Enoch nodded and asked, "Do you think you handled that the best way, Son?"

"I couldn't take anymore, Father!" he said emphatically. "I tried, I really did try not to fight, but when they hit her with the basket, I had to do something! They weren't going to leave us alone until I did." Then, looking at his mother with all the feigned seriousness he could muster, "Besides, they threw Mother's honeybread into the pond."

Ednah couldn't help herself as she let out a little chuckle. "My hero!" she said.

Enoch just looked at both of them and shook his head. "I suppose you did your best to avoid the fight, but sometimes it can be nearly impossible when the other party insists on it. It is getting late, Son. You better get some sleep. We have a lot of work to do tomorrow. We need to get started on our late summer crops. There's a lot of plowing to be done. I know it won't live up to your level of excitement, but it's all I can come up with for now, " he said with a sideways smile.

Methuselah yawned and turned to go to his room, "That's alright. I'll try and spice it up a bit."

~~

It was late afternoon the next day when Enoch and Methuselah had finished plowing and were watering the oxen. Enoch stood to stretch his back and wipe his brow when he noticed a man on a horse coming down the path toward the house. "Who do you suppose that is, Methuselah?" he asked his son.

Methuselah watched for a moment and, with a surprised look, answered, "I believe that is Ando, who works for Tamari's father. I hope there's no trouble."

As Ando rode into the yard, he stepped down from his horse and approached where the two men were working. "Greetings from the house of Jaylon," he said.

"Greetings," said Enoch as he and Methuselah were wiping their hands and trying to look more presentable for the well-dressed messenger. "What can we do for you Ando?"

"Jaylon and Naamah have asked me to come and ask a favor of you; actually, a few favors of you. First, she will be entertaining some very important guests tomorrow, and Naamah asked, if it wouldn't be too much trouble, that your wife would bake her four loaves of her famous honeybread?"

"No trouble at all," said Ednah, who had heard the horse trotting into the yard and came out to see what was happening. "Will four be enough?"

"Oh, yes," he said, surprised she was behind him. "That is all she will require. Of course, she will pay you handsomely for it."

Ednah raised her hands and said, "Tell her that it is an honor for her to want to serve my bread to such important guests. Also, tell her that I will be sending eight loaves so that she will have plenty. I will send a few for you as well, Ando."

"You are too kind. I am sure it will be greatly appreciated," Ando said. "Secondly, Jaylon is having trouble with his fish grinder and asked if Methuselah could come tomorrow with the bread and look at it? He seems to have a knack for these things. There seems to be something binding it up and we need to get the fish slurry into the soil before the late summer planting. We are already behind schedule."

Enoch put his hand on Methuselah's back and responded with a smile, "We are happy to be of help to Jaylon. Methuselah will be there at midmorning with the bread and will also look at that fish grinder for him. Is there anything else we can do for you, Ando?"

"No, thank you. You and your family have been most gracious already. Have a pleasant evening." With that, he bowed and mounted his horse to leave.

"Oh, Methuselah, Jaylon said to wear something that you will not mind getting dirty. The fish grinder is very messy and I'm afraid you won't smell very good when you're done," Ando added as he started trotting back down the trail.

Methuselah looked at his father, who was in deep thought, "Father, though I don't really want to fool with that fish grinder tomorrow, it would seem that Tamari's father must not be too upset with me for her getting home so late last night. Perhaps he has changed his mind about me after hearing how I defended her from those oafs. Perhaps this will be my chance to show him that I'm not so bad after all."

"Perhaps, Methuselah," Enoch said as he rubbed his chin thoughtfully. Something bothered Enoch about this, but he wasn't sure what it was. The timing was strange. Jaylon had never reached out to him for any help before now. Also, a fish grinder wasn't a very technical piece of machinery. Surely, he had other workers there that could fix it for him. But perhaps Jaylon was indeed trying to give Methuselah a chance to prove himself. He prayed so.

Chapter 7

METHUSELAH AWOKE EXCITED ABOUT WHAT THIS DAY WOULD bring for him. He would see his beloved Tamari today, which always gladdened his heart. Also, he was going to start a new chapter in the somewhat strained relationship he and her father had had up to this point. Methuselah had convinced himself that Tamari's father had been told of his heroic defense of her and would give him a fresh chance to prove himself if not outright thank him. In his mind, this would be a good day.

As he lay there thinking about all this, the aroma of baking bread invaded his senses. "Was there ever a smell so wonderful?" he asked himself. He could stay in bed no longer. His stomach growled its desires, and he had to taste it for himself. He stretched and moaned, yawning loudly to announce to anyone in the house that he was astir.

His little sister, Mirah, heard his announcement and responded to it immediately with a squeal, "Mefusa awake! Mefusa awake, Mama!" She then bounded into the room with an explosion of excitement. She ran at full speed and jumped up into the not-so-expectant stomach of her brother. He grunted and laughed simultaneously, beaming at the loving little ball of energy.

"Good morning, little one. What's made you so happy this morning?" Methuselah asked as he tickled her chubby belly. This, of course, elicited another squeal of delight and more laughter.

"Mama bake bed!" she replied. Then, she made the overdramatic motions of someone smelling something delicious.

Methuselah loved this little bundle of pure, sweet love. Mirah had brought much laughter into the house and their lives, and, at times such as this, he couldn't help but overflow with the joy of her brightness and laughter.

Then, without warning, he picked her up and carried her like a sack under his arm into the kitchen, where his mother stood smiling at the sight of the two of them having such fun with each other. Mirah squealed her approval the whole way.

"Are you ready to have some breakfast? There are more berries and some pomegranate over there with a half a loaf of fresh bread," said his mother pointing to the opposite counter.

"Yes," he said. "I couldn't take much more of that smell without having some. The house smells so good when you're baking." He then shoved a large piece of bread into his mouth and sloppily chewed it before continuing with his mouth half full. "Where is Father this morning? He isn't in the field, is he? We finished the late summer planting yesterday."

His mother gave a little sigh and shook her head. "No, he said he needed to go for a walk. Something seems to be troubling him this morning, but he wouldn't tell me what it was. He only said he needed to talk with the Lord about it."

Enoch was at the northern end of his little valley up on the low mountain that fed the river and, in turn, watered his farm. He liked to come here from time to time, feeling that he was able to get a better perspective on his life. He could look out over his little world and think, thank, pray, or shout; whichever was needed at the time to help him with what might be happening in that beautiful dell he called home. He wasn't sure which of these he would be doing today.

He had been troubled by Jaylon's request for his son. It didn't make sense to him that Jaylon would need Methuselah to fix something that any of his servants could have fixed. He tried to take Methuselah's tack on this, but it didn't fit with what he knew of Tamari's father. Jaylon had been a good man when he was a farmer and could be counted on to generally do the right thing in most cases. However, since he had discovered those emeralds, he had become a wholly different person, and for that matter, so had his wife. Where they were content with the simple life of a farmer before, now, they seemed preoccupied with gaining notoriety and status among the city's elites. They just couldn't be bothered with the simple people of the valleys anymore.

As Enoch pondered these things, a voice broke through the silence. "Hello, my child. Tell Me of your troubles," said the Lord incarnate.

"Oh, Creator of all, I am humbled by your love and concern for a lowly sinner such as me! You alone are truly worthy of my praise!" Enoch immediately dropped and bowed low before the Lord.

"Stand up, my faithful," the Lord responded with a smile. "We have much to discuss."

Enoch slowly rose and took in the sight of this perfect being. He would never get used to these glorious visitations from the Lord. Every time, it would nearly stop his heart; so awesome was this Holiest's countenance. He had flawless skin that glowed with the glory of perfection. His hair was brown and a bit wavy as it fell lightly to His shoulders. He was the same height as Enoch but had the most unusual eyes. They would be one color at one moment but then change with the emotion of the conversation. When the Lord spoke of His love, they would be the deepest blue. When He spoke of His authority, they would be a golden or purple shade. But, when He spoke of the anger that burned for those who disobeyed His will, they would take on the look of burning fire and could strip away any thought of self. Enoch would tremble and worship at those times, fearing that those burning eyes would be directed at him.

Today, however, His eyes had a greenish hue and seemed somewhat sad. This brought worry to Enoch's heart.

"What, my Lord, can Your humble servant do to please You today?" said Enoch with his hands in a pleading gesture.

"Enoch, my son, your heart has been troubled by the occurrences of the past few days," the Lord said. "I have put this in your heart so that you would react just as you have. You need to pray for Tamari. She is going to go through a time of great distress. Her faith is strong by way of the example you and your family have shown her, but it will be tested greatly. And also shall the faith of Methuselah be tested. Pray that he remain strong in his faith and wise in his dealings. Pray that he will learn the value of forgiveness toward his enemies. This will be required of him very soon if he is to have what his heart desires."

"Also," the Lord continued. "You were asked to perform a task for Me many years ago and were told to keep this task a secret until the appointed time. Do you remember this?"

Enoch thought for a moment, then realization crossed his face, "You speak of the injured giant, Gardan. Yes, Lord, I remember."

The Creator nodded. "It will soon be time to reap your reward for this act of kindness. The seeds of love that you sowed into his heart are almost ready to sprout forth. Follow the river south until you find him. Before you leave, you should tell Ednah not to allow Methuselah and the others to go on their search until you return with Gardan."

"Search?" Enoch asked. "What would we be searching for?"

"You will know when you return with Gardan. Through all that is about to happen, you should be fearless and faithful. I am in control. I will be there with you. Remember, I, and I alone, hold the keys to life. Through Me, all things are possible."

With that, the Creator was gone. Enoch spent the next two hours praying for his son, Tamari, and for the wisdom to stay faithful no matter what the days to come would bring. Then, he returned to his house to give Ednah the message for Methuselah and prepare for the trip to get his large friend.

Chapter 8

THE HOME OF JAYLON WAS ABUZZ WITH THE PREPARATIONS FOR today's feast. The best fruits and vegetables were spread over the large table in the expansive dining hall. Servants were busy cleaning everything to a fine degree and washing the cedarwood floors so that they would shine. Naamah was running the process with precision. She had entertained many prominent guests in the past few years, but none more so than today's guests.

Leader Bertlaw was the chief supplier of metals in Urna and had become quite wealthy over the years. Over the past three years, however, he had introduced strange new tools to the people of the city. These new tools were meant for something other than farming, though. They were meant for protection, as he had put it. The city fathers had taken to these tools quite quickly. As a result, Bertlaw had become ever more prominent in the ranks of the city leaders.

He had traveled east to the cities of Nod to learn of this new technology. When he returned, he carried samples of the swords and shields that would allow their city to protect it and its citizens from the marauding bands of raiders that had started to form in the north.

Only once had these so-called marauders come to Urna and had only set fire to the home of one of its citizens. This man was also known to have wronged the people of the northern villages in a business deal. But the facts didn't seem to get in the way of the city leaders' decision to start the formation of an army.

Bertlaw had volunteered some of his lands to build the army's training center and supplied the needed swords and shields. This, he did for a nominal fee, of course, and the prestigious place at the head of the table of the city leaders' council. As a result, he wielded great power and influence in Urna and the surrounding areas.

Bertlaw's wife, Zillah, immensely enjoyed the attention she received as one of the city elites. She would have the city's most elaborate parties and feasts. She was infamously known to ridicule and scoff at the people she considered beneath her. She would often invite one of these lesser people to her parties to embarrass them in front of her sycophantic friends. But, to turn down the invitation to one of these cruel events would mean that you wouldn't be getting any more business from the city by way of her husband, whose ear she had full access to. She, in her own way, held as much, if not more, power than her husband.

Naamah knew precisely what type of people they were but was determined to impress them by whatever means necessary. It was no small thing to have Bertlaw and his wife come to her home; she would not squander this opportunity.

She called for the finest clothiers in Urna and sent her servants all over the surrounding areas to gather the most beautiful and fragrant flowers that could be found. She had these flowers fashioned into laurels to decorate her daughters' hair and the most fragrant ones for use in a perfumed bath in which to soak the girls. She was determined to add to the natural beauty already possessed by Tamari and Julis. In her mind, the son of Bertlaw would have no choice but to fall instantly in love with one of these girls. Hopefully, it would be Tamari. Then, she could leave the thoughts of that grubby farm boy in the past.

Methuselah happily walked down the path to Tamari's house with a tune whistling from his lips. This was the day he had hoped for. Today he would be able to show himself worthy of Tamari's love. His head was full of these idealistic thoughts. He had practiced his speech and revised it several times. He would win her father over to his side of things. How could Jaylon not see that he was the man for his daughter after he had protected her from the advances of a mannerless oaf like Rimlah?

As Methuselah entered the spacious yard, he was struck by the size of the house. Before Jaylon had found the emeralds on his land, they had a much smaller home than this one. In fact, it was slightly smaller than the one that Methuselah had grown up in. Within a matter of a month, they were building this new home. They had decided to build this one more in the fashion of the homes of the wealthier people in the city.

They had leveled a large portion of their farmland and lain large polished river rocks out into a courtyard that encircled the entire house. Inside the courtyards were small gardens with beautiful flowers attracting the hummingbirds that Tamari and Julis loved to watch dance about. The house itself had many large rooms for every purpose. An entryway with hanging plants led into a formal dining room decorated with more plants and ornately sculptured cedar tables. There was a large kitchen area and a servant's area for the more unpleasant tasks of the household. The other half of the house was reserved for the bedrooms. Off the dining room were large open windows with delicate drapes that could be opened or shut quickly to give a view of the small valley and large birdbaths in the rear courtyard. To Methuselah, it was all a bit much, but everyone had their tastes.

"Methuselah!" said Ando coming from the sideyard. "Over here. Let me introduce you to Dolan. He will be assisting you with the fish grinder. Oh, I see you also have the bread from your mother," he said as he took the basket from him. "Oh, that smells so good. Your mother is the best bread-maker anywhere around."

They walked toward the rear of the house, where a rather plump man was speaking to one of the house servants. Methuselah noticed they hushed their conversation when he came close enough to hear but thought nothing of it. "Dolan," said Ando. "This is Methuselah. His father was the man who invented that fish grinder. If anyone can help you fix it, he can."

Dolan nodded his hello and started walking toward the barn where the grinder was kept.

"Not much for conversation, I guess," Methuselah said as he watched the man unceremoniously leave him standing there.

Ando just shrugged his shoulders and shook his head, "I guess not. He seems to be in a mood today. Perhaps it's because you were called in when he couldn't get it fixed. Just go with him if you will and he will show you what is going on with the grinder." With that, Ando turned and directed a man with some flowers to take them to another door.

"I hope you don't think I'm trying to show anyone up or anything like that. I was asked to come and help with this today," Methuselah said as he entered the barn behind the man.

Dolan looked at him and shook his head, "No, it's nothing like that. There are just so many people here today that I don't know. I get nervous around new people."

"I understand," said Methuselah with a wave of his hand. "Now, what's going on with this contraption?" he asked, turning his attention to the problematic machine.

After one of his walks, his father came up with the idea of mixing ground-up fish into the soil. It was a bizarre idea at the time. The soil had been rich enough to yield a good harvest for many years, but with time the yields had dwindled to almost half of their original output. Also, the size of the fruits and vegetables he grew had gradually reduced, year after year.

Then, he went to Bertlaw and showed him a drawing of this new fish grinding machine he wanted him to construct. It was a simple device consisting of a hopper on top that would funnel the fish down into a tube with a screw that, when turned, would break the fish into smaller pieces and force them through a plate with holes in it. What came out was a chunky slurry of fishmeal and fish guts.

Everyone thought Enoch was crazy until he came to town after the next season to share his results. His yield nearly doubled along with the size of the fruit and vegetables. With the proof staring them in the face, there was no denying that his idea would also benefit the other farmers. He then asked Bertlaw to make one for every farmer in the area. Bertlaw said that there was an obvious profit to be made from this new invention, but Enoch wanted no payment for his idea. He wanted his neighbors to gain freely for themselves from the goodness of the Creator's love. In the end, though, Bertlaw had decided to charge four times what he had charged Enoch for the original machine. It was only fitting, he said, that he should make a little something for his efforts in helping his neighbors.

Now, looking at the disgusting-smelling machine, Methuselah could not immediately see the problem. He tried to turn the screw. It wouldn't budge. He thought for a moment before speaking, "Have you tried taking it apart to see if something is caught in it and stopping it up?"

"Our tools for it broke when we tried," said Dolan, holding up the wrench with a missing side. "Did you bring the one for your grinder?"

Methuselah shook his head and thought about the problem, "No, but if you have some strong string and small planks of wood we can fashion something that worked well for us when ours got stuck like this once."

After a while, they found what they needed and went to work, trying to make a new wrench. They tied two slats of sturdy wood to the square nut on the back of the screw, one on either side. Then found another piece of wood that would slip between the two already on the nut. With a bit of whittling, it fit snugly. Then, Methuselah gently tugged on the newly fashioned wrench. At first, he thought it wouldn't be strong enough to hold, but slowly, the nut started to turn until it gave way entirely and could be loosened by hand.

"That was a very good idea you had there," said Dolan. "It's no wonder they called you in to help."

"Well, that is only part of it. Now we have to find out what's keeping the screw from turning," Methuselah said.

He gave the screw a tug to pull it out, but it wouldn't budge. He pulled harder and got the same results. Then, bracing his feet on the legs of the table upon which the heavy machine sat, he jerked it with all his might. It finally let loose and sent him flying back into the trough where some of the fish slurry had formed a pool, waiting to be released down the hill and into the fields.

Dolan couldn't help but laugh a bit at the sight of Methuselah struggling to escape the trough. Dolan then reached out his hand and helped him out, "You're going to smell for a while. That is a hard smell to get out of your clothes, as well as your skin and hair."

Looking at himself, Methuselah had to laugh, "These are old work clothes anyway, but you're right about the rest. I hope Tamari doesn't see me like this."

Dolan gave him an odd glance and then smiled, "Yes, that would be rather embarrassing I would think. You might as well finish the job before cleaning up. It may get messy for you again."

"Let's hope not," said Methuselah wryly.

As he examined the screw, he saw that something like pitch was stuck to the whole thing and seemed to get thicker toward the plate at the end. He reached in and pulled at the plate, and it slowly released itself from the end of the tube. It, too, was caked with the sticky substance.

He took a deep breath saying, "I think we have our work cut out for us. This could take a while to get out of here." Then he looked over at Dolan. "Why would someone put pitch in here? I can't see any reason for it."

Dolan just shrugged and shook his head. "I don't know. Perhaps someone was angry with Jaylon and wanted to get him back somehow. He has been a little harsh with some of the servants. Anyway, I'll try to find something we can use to scrape this gunk out of here." He went into a small tool room and returned with two scraping tools. "We can start with these."

After hours of soaking, Tamari and her sister, Julis, were finally allowed to get out of the perfumed bath. Julis liked to be pampered this way. She would spend hours dressing in her mother's fine tunics and robes. She would wear her ornate jewelry and pin her curly brown hair up in the fashion of the elite women of the cities. She would then dance and prance around, acting like she was the center of attention for an imaginary crowd of admirers, thanking them for their imaginary compliments.

Tamari, on the other hand, was simpler in her tastes. She liked to wear pretty things but confidently carried herself and didn't need the frills and trappings of the wealthy to gain admirers. Her classic, natural beauty was clear enough for that. However, today her mother wouldn't have her relying on her God-given attributes. She wanted Tamari to have the entire arsenal of womanly guiles to throw at this special courtier.

Tamari wasn't told who would be coming to her house today. She was only told that she needed to look her best. She was told that before but had never been subjected to this much scrutiny and attention for such a visit. In fact, an emissary for King Seth had even visited to acquire emeralds for the king's treasury, and she had only been told to wear her finest tunic and fix her hair nicely. She wondered who this visitor could be to warrant more respect than the king's emissary.

Now, after being dressed in the frilliest and most elaborate tunics, scarves, and shoes they had ever seen, the girls' hair was brushed, teased, and adorned with gold and jewels. Then, they were affixed with flowered laurels that coiled around and through their hair, then flowed regally down to the middle of their backs.

The clothiers then stepped back and wore looks of immense pride as they surveyed their work. They gently ushered Tamari and Julis toward the polished silver mirror in the corner of the dressing room. When she saw herself, Julis squealed with delight and spun to and fro, beaming with awe at how stunning she appeared.

Tamari stood in shock. She had never seen herself this way, and though she wasn't given to self-admiration, she felt like she had never looked this beautiful. The white and pink orchids that lazily flowed down through her hair perfectly accentuated her bright green eyes and strawberry-blonde locks. She immediately wondered what Methuselah's reaction would be if he were to see her now. This thought brought a broad smile to her face.

"Oh, Tamari," Julis said, bubbling with glee. "I wish Jubal and Methuselah could see us now! Their jaws would simply fall off their faces."

"I know," said Tamari. "I only hope to look this good on my wedding day."

Naamah, hearing the excited squeal of her youngest daughter, came rushing into the room and stopped cold in her tracks. With her hands to her mouth, a tear came to her eye as she gazed pridefully at these two visions of feminine beauty.

"Oh, my girls look so beautiful! Our guests are going to faint at the sight of you two," said their mother, almost singing the words. "Come with me. I want your father to see you."

She ushered them out into the dining hall, where their father was surveying the final preparations for the feast.

Naamah excitedly called for Jaylon's attention, saying, "Jaylon, I present to you, Princess Tamari and Princess Julis." She waved her hand toward the entrance and backed away to clear the view for their father as the girls entered the room. All in the room nearly stopped breathing at the sight of them, Jaylon included.

"My two daughters are more beautiful than any jewels I have ever seen. It is not even close. Jewels have flaws, where, before me now, I can see none." He walked over, kissed them each on the cheek, and smelled the flowers in their hair.

"Don't the flowers make them look so pretty?" said their mother.

Jaylon shook his head. "No, my dear, these two young women make the flowers look pretty."

The girls giggled and blushed a bit. Their father could be quite charming sometimes, and both the girls loved it when he showered them with compliments. Since he had started mining gems, he spent less time with them. Therefore, he also hadn't given them many of those most sought-after compliments his daughters needed to hear. This one brought tears to their eyes as they each rewarded him with a hug.

As they composed themselves, the announcement came from a servant outside that their guests had arrived. This sent everyone into a flurry of activity to make a final check to be sure everything was perfect. Jaylon took Naamah's hand and led her to the front courtyard to greet them as they arrived. Having been through all this before, the girls followed behind to take their respective places beside them.

As they stood regally awaiting them, Tamari wondered again who this could be that so much pomp was warranted. The procession that came slowly into view was, indeed, impressive. First, the finely dressed soldiers were walking in lock-step with each other with their shimmering bronze swords and shields. Then came the horsemen pulling the ornate covered cart that held the esteemed guests, who were obviously of great wealth and importance. They were followed by no less than eight servants dressed in finely tailored uniforms and carrying all manner of items so as to give supreme comfort to their masters in any circumstance that should arise.

Tamari thought that perhaps it was King Seth himself, given all the pageantry and the accompanying soldiers. This guest was, indeed, important.

The procession finally came to a halt at the edge of the courtyard, and a servant with a small set of steps went to the door of the covered carriage. He sat them down, stepped to the side, and opened the door. Another servant rushed up with a sizeable bird-feather sunshade and extended a hand toward the occupant, who was now emerging from the carriage. The girls exchanged a quick glance with each other, anxious to see who would step out.

The woman took the hand of the servant and gingerly came down the steps with the grace of a queen. She was a pretty woman, finely dressed and bejeweled with gold, rubies, and emeralds from head to hand. She was slightly plump but carried it well. She walked a few steps into the courtyard without even glancing at the awaiting hosts and turned to wait for her husband, who was now stepping to the ground. He was obviously well-fed and wore many rings and a thick gold necklace. He joined his wife and turned to wait for a third occupant.

Her heart almost stopped when Tamari saw who stepped out of the carriage next. She said an almost involuntary "No!" before she could stop herself. Her mother spun her head and grabbed her hand, then sank her fingernails into her skin.

Naamah quickly and quietly whispered, "What is the matter with you? You better be on your best behavior." Then she turned back to her guests and put her best fake smile back on her face.

Tamari couldn't believe she had spent so much time getting perfumed, dressed up, and fixed up for this stupid oaf. She wanted to turn and run. She wanted to scream. Anything would be better than being forced to be nice to Rimlah for the afternoon. He repulsed her like no one had ever before. However, she would have to try her best for her father's sake. She was nearly nauseous over it, but it was only one afternoon. Besides, she would just avoid him until the dinner was over.

Once all together, the guests turned and made their way toward the awaiting hosts. When the man was introduced to the girls, he took their hands and bowed slightly. "Lovely to meet you both," he said. Then the woman did the same. When it came time for the introduction to Rimlah, Tamari couldn't even hear what was said due to her heartbeat pounding in her ears. She offered her hand and politely, though half-heartedly, nodded hello. It was all she could do not to scream.

They all went inside. Tamari stood for a moment outside the door, looking out at the tall grasses in the fields. She wondered if she could hide within those grasses long enough to avoid having to see or speak to Rimlah this afternoon. She laughed slightly at the thought, took a deep breath, and went on into the house.

She spent the next few hours trying desperately to avoid Rimlah, which was no small feat. It was beginning to dawn on her that this whole party seemed to be centered on her and Rimlah. Whenever he came close to her, she would find a reason to retreat to the other side of the room. No sooner had she found relative safety when her mother or father would call her back to where Rimlah was telling of some uninteresting tidbit of news about himself, or she was being urged to do the same about herself. The longer this went on, the more obvious it became. The more obvious it became, the angrier she was getting. She prayed that this would end soon.

———

Methuselah and Dolan finally finished scraping the pitch out of the fish grinder and its parts and got it put back together. It had taken three hours of intense scraping, and both men were glad to be done with it.

"Alright," said Methuselah. "Let's try this thing out and see if we can get some fish through it. Do you have any fish ready to go?"

"Yes, right over here," said Dolan. "First, let's see if it looks clear. I'll turn it without any fish in it. You look at the plate and check that it's working right." Dolan had netted some fish the day before and had them sitting out in the sun before Methuselah arrived. As Methuselah bent down to look closely at the plate, Dolan picked up the bucket of nasty fish and dumped them in the hopper.

Methuselah was waiting to see the screw turn through the holes in the plate when his open eyes were suddenly awash in rancid fish water.

"Aaaah!" he screamed as the disgusting water flooded his eyes, mouth, and nose. "What did you do that for?"

"I'm sorry. I guess I misunderstood what you wanted me to do," said Dolan. "Hurry, take my hand, and I'll take you to wash that out of your eyes." He took Methuselah's hand and led him to the large birdbath just outside of the dining hall. His eyes were burning from the filthy fish tea as he blindly dug for the water in the bath.

Dolan stepped back out of sight next to the draped window and spoke in a thunderous voice. "Methuselah, I bet that burns!"

Suddenly, the drapes to the large window opening were parted widely. Methuselah heard this and turned to see through still half-blind eyes that a room full of finely dressed people was watching him as he tried to wash the nasty concoction out of his eyes and mouth. He grabbed another few handfuls of water to finish clearing his sight. Finally, it came into focus.

The people in the house started laughing hysterically and pointing in his direction. "Look at the grubby farm boy trying to wash himself in a bird bath!" yelled the plump woman next to Tamari's mother, reveling at the sight of his embarrassment. Jaylon was next to her, doing the same thing. Then, he saw Tamari standing next to, of all people, Rimlah. She looked shocked as a tear ran down her cheek.

Methuselah was in absolute turmoil, overtaken by all the moment's emotions. He was surprised, embarrassed, hurt, humiliated, and irate all at once. His mind froze. What was he to do? What could he say? Finally, his legs did the only thing they knew to do; they ran.

All the people continued laughing at the pitiful sight of the dirty little farm boy running scared; everyone but Tamari and Julis, as they were fully surprised by what had just occurred. Tamari turned to her mother and father with a look of utter contempt.

"You see?" her mother said. "That is all he will ever be; a farm boy. Look at yourself. Is that really all you think you deserve when you can do so much better?" This last part, she said while motioning in Rimlah's direction.

Tamari's eyes welled up with giant tears, and she ran out of the dining hall and into her room, slamming the heavy wooden door behind her.

Chapter 9

METHUSELAH RAN BACK UP THE PATH TOWARD THE LOW PASS in the hills between Tamari's house and his, muttering indecipherably to himself the entire way. Between curses against Tamari's parents, the fat woman, Dolan, Rimlah, and whoever else may have conspired to make him the butt of this cruel joke, he kept asking himself a question. "What just happened back there? Why did they do that when I was just trying to help?" He waved his arms around and shook his fists toward the cursed people's house as it grew smaller in the distance while he gained elevation on the hill. He stopped at the pond where they had eaten their picnic a few days before and jumped into the water to wash the now-drying fish slurry off of himself.

The cool water helped him to calm down a bit. He was still furious, but he was also something very much worse; heart-broken. "Why would Tamari have been there with Rimlah of all people? She knows how much I despise him." He started to weep but fought it back again with the anger he was feeling. He was now using the mud in the pond to try and scrub the rotten fish smell out of his skin, but he was barely conscious of what he was doing.

"Methuselah, are you talking to yourself?" asked Jubal, who had just walked up as Methuselah was asking himself that last question.

A bit startled, Methuselah spun around, but when he saw who was there, he went back to what he was doing and answered, "Yes, I guess I am Jubal. *Apparently*, it's safer than talking to anyone else. I'm not going to try and embarrass myself like *other* people might." This he said in a very sarcastic tone.

"What are you talking about?" asked Jubal. "Who tried to embarrass you?"

Jubal listened in stunned disbelief as Methuselah recounted the whole story to him. He interrupted a few times to get a little more detail but mostly listened like a good friend would. He waited until he had told the whole tale before giving any opinions on the matter. Even then, Jubal let a few long moments pass before saying anything.

Finally, with a deep sigh, he spoke, "Methuselah, I am so sorry that happened to you today, but what doesn't make sense is that Tamari was with Rimlah at that party or...whatever it was. She can hardly stand him. Perhaps it was Jaylon who invited his parents over and Tamari had no choice but to be there. Just because they were in the same house together doesn't mean they were together. She has always been good and honest with you. I'm sure there's a good explanation for what you saw."

"I'm telling you, Jubal, she stood right next to him. She was dressed up nicer than I have ever seen. She has never gotten so dressed up for *me* like that," snapped Methuselah. "If you had only seen what I saw then you wouldn't be so quick to take up for her. You should have seen it. They were just having a grand time laughing it up at the poor little farmer boy. I swear, I should have taught that little rich boy a lesson when I had the chance the other day!"

Jubal just listened and let Methuselah vent his anger. He made no more comments or excuses. He just listened, then walked back home with him when he had finished bathing, saying only, "Methuselah, you still smell like fish."

Methuselah smiled for the first time since the episode happened. He loved his friend and cousin, Jubal. He always seemed to be there when Methuselah needed him.

⌒

"Tamari?" asked the voice at the door. It was the voice of her mother. It had been an hour since the incident, and Tamari had had a chance to scream some anger and frustration into her pillow. Still, she felt used and hurt by the owner of the voice that was now at her door and didn't feel like talking to her.

"Tamari, we need to talk, dear," said Naamah as she pushed through the door.

Tamari was sitting on her bed, arms folded, looking directly ahead as her mother approached her. She had never been one to be angry with anyone for very long, but she was determined to try her best to stay angry today.

"Tamari, I know you are upset right now, but we have guests and we cannot allow you to be rude to them any longer. We let you come in here and pout for a while, but you need to get up, fix your face, and be a gracious host. These are very important guests and we don't want to have to make any excuses for our willful daughter who is acting like a four-year-old who hasn't gotten her way."

Tamari turned and scowled at her mother. She couldn't believe what she had just heard. "*Why*, Mother? Why did you do that to Methuselah? What has he done so wrong that you would embarrass him that way? He and his family have been nothing but polite to you and Father, but you never have one nice thing to say about them. Why is that, Mother?"

Her mother took a deep breath and answered, "Dear, it's not that we hate them. I'm sure they are nice people, but they aren't the standard of people that you need to associate yourself with. They are mere farmers, but you deserve a prince."

"Mother," said Tamari, looking straight into her mother's eyes, "until about three years ago, *we* were mere farmers. Do you not remember, Mother? I remember when Father was sick, and it was Enoch and Methuselah who came to help us harvest our crops. Were they the '*right standard of people*' then?"

Naamah's eyes widened with anger, and she slapped her across the face. "You do not speak to me that way! I am only trying to give you the best that life has to offer. Now, you get yourself cleaned up and get out there. I'll not wait long." Then, she left the room, only to rejoin the party with a laugh as if something funny was happening in the room she had just left.

Tamari hated how her mother acted around people she thought were important. She had heard that same fake laugh so many times that it almost made her physically ill. She longed for the days when they were still "mere farmers." Life was so much better then. Now, everything was about appearances to her parents. She was to appear happy whether she was or not, and now, she is expected to do it again. "Fine," she thought to herself. "If that is what I must do to help get this evening over with, fine."

As the afternoon went on, she did her best to act happy, but it was useless. She could only manage to twitch a smile here and there. She was miserable, and a small part of her wanted everyone to know it. Her only consolation was that Rimlah, seeing how miserable she was, had finally stopped trying to talk to her. It wasn't much, but she would take what she could get.

A while later, just before they were about to leave, Rimlah cautiously approached her with an understanding expression on his face.

"Tamari, I'm sorry that happened earlier," he said so sincerely that it caught her off guard a bit. He continued, "Methuselah and I have had our differences, but that *was* a rather cruel and insensitive thing to do to someone. I can only imagine how that must have felt." Then, with a bow of the head, "Well, actually,

I'm sure I can relate to some degree. That was how I felt the other day at the pond."

Not quite sure what to think of this new side of Rimlah, she relented a slight smile, "I guess you were a bit embarrassed, weren't you?"

He gave a sheepish look and continued, "I want you to know that I was going to stand down and let you go, but my idiot friends wanted to push the issue. I really didn't want you to get into any trouble. I hope I didn't cause you too much grief."

She gave him a stern look, "Well, you did cause me grief. My father yelled at me and blamed Methuselah for my being so late. You can blame it on your idiot friends if you like, but we both know they were only following your lead. Your friends got what they were asking for, but Methuselah had pity on you. A lot more pity than anyone, including your mother, showed him today."

With that, she turned and left him standing there with his mouth agape.

There were no more words spoken between them that afternoon. Bertlaw and his family left, and as soon as their carriage got out of sight, she returned to her room. She didn't speak another word for the rest of the night. She only thought of Methuselah and wished she could hold him and tell him how sorry she was for how her parents had treated him. She fell asleep that night with tears for Methuselah on her pillow.

"I think we were a bit too cruel to Methuselah today," said Jaylon sitting on the edge of the bed. "The idea was to make her not like him anymore, but I think we may have made her hate *us* instead."

Naamah approached her husband and put her hands on his shoulders, rubbing them gently, "Jaylon, my dearest, she will never hate us. She will be angry for a time, but we are her parents. A child is supposed to be angry with her parents when she is corrected, but eventually, she will understand that what we do is for her own good."

Jaylon thought for a moment, "Naamah, she is hardly a child anymore. I wonder if we are doing the right thing interfering in her emotions. I want the best for her, but if she is not happy, is it the best for her after all?"

"Don't give up yet, my dear husband," said his wife with a mischievous smirk. "Don't give up yet. A young girl's heart can be fickle. Sometimes you just have to give her more time to change her mind."

Chapter 10

WHEN METHUSELAH AND JUBAL ARRIVED AT THE HOUSE THE day before, his mother was acting strangely. She asked if everyone was alright. This, in itself, was not so strange. His mother often worried about everyone's safety like any mother would. Methuselah thought she might have sensed something was wrong when he came home upset and smelling like rotten fish. But, after he told her what had happened, she asked if everyone else was alright. He wondered why she would be so concerned for the people who had caused him so much grief. Then she asked if anyone was missing. When he said no, she was somewhat relieved and told him to stay close to the house and not leave until his father got home.

He was used to her being overly concerned, but Methuselah thought this to be a bizarre line of questioning. When he pressed her for a reason, she only said he needed to stay put until his father got home. She prayed that whole evening and spent more hours in prayer the next day. She was truly upset about something but wouldn't tell him what it was. This caused him to pray too. He wasn't sure what he was praying for, but to worry his mother like that, whatever it was, must be important. So, he prayed.

Tamari awoke to the sound of her mother's calling, "Tamari, Julis, it's time to get up and eat some breakfast. We have things to do today."

Tamari stretched and looked toward her sister's bed to see Julis getting dressed into another of her prettier tunics. "Julis, what are we supposed to be doing today?"

Julis shrugged her shoulders. "I'm not entirely sure, but we *are* going into Urna. That is all I know. Mother said to get into something pretty. How does this look?" she asked, turning from side to side.

"It looks fine," answered Tamari as she swung her feet to the floor and wiggled her toes.

She didn't want to go into Urna today. She wanted to stay home and continue being angry. She also wanted to go see Methuselah. She tried to be understanding about her parent's behavior. Still, when she thought about how Methuselah must have felt, she would get angry again. She sure didn't feel like being around them today, but apparently, she had no choice. Her only course of retaliation would be not speaking to them. Her mother wouldn't have much problem with that, but her father, who couldn't stand it for very long, would usually relent and apologize for whatever he had done, sometimes even if it wasn't his fault.

With a deep breath and a sigh, Tamari finally resigned herself to the fate she was handed for this day and got dressed. As was her custom of late, she would get through it the best she could.

The trip to Urna in the simple horse-drawn carriage was relatively uneventful. Naamah talked about how she wanted a carriage like the one in which Leader Bertlaw and his family had arrived the day before. She carried on about the style of clothing Bertlaw's wife, Zillah, had worn. Then she spoke about all the stunning jewelry Zillah had worn. She went on and on about how she wanted to be like Zillah.

Jaylon, who could take no more of this incessant banter from his wife, turned and interrupted her in mid-sentence, "Do you also want to be fat as a melon like your idol, Zillah? Please stop going on about how you want to look like *Zillah!*"

He then looked over to see the steely stare he was getting from his wife and decided to try to save himself. "What I mean to say is that she dresses too flashy. You, however, don't need to dress that way to get attention. Your beauty stands on its own without the need for such gaudy dress."

The two girls tried to stifle their giggles at these proceedings, but a few escaped them anyway. This brought the same icy stare their father had just received back to them. Then she looked back to Jaylon, who had a sheepishly assuring expression on his face. It was a relatively weak attempt at appeasing her. Still, the way it came out was comical enough that it elicited a slight smirk of a smile out of Naamah.

"You think you're so funny. I know I don't *need* all those things," she said. "I was merely admiring them." Then, folding her arms, she looked off at the passing scenery, undoubtedly pouting. Jaylon looked over at her, then stole another look back to Tamari and Julis, who were still trying not to laugh at the comical scene that was taking place before them. He gave a wry little grin and looked back to the road.

As they entered the city of Urna, they all took note of the progress being made on the city's defensive walls, which were now about two-thirds complete. The walls were the suggestion of Leader Bertlaw when he started to train the city's new soldiers. He had said that it would be a deterrent against attack and would be another way to "ensure the safety of his fellow Urnians." Most of the people within the city were happy with it. They wanted to avoid being seen as behind the times by the people of other nearby cities who had also built up their city's defenses against these heretofore unseen attackers. Others in the city and the surrounding farmers thought that the wall made it seem as though the city had something valuable inside to protect and, therefore, was inviting the very attacks the wall was supposed to be guarding against. Both sides of the debate were argued and politicked, but the final decision was to be made by Leader Bertlaw. He made his decision, and the results were plainly seen rising up all around the city.

"This used to be an inviting little city," Jaylon said to himself as they approached the still-unfinished city gates. "Now, it's as if Urna either doesn't want anyone to enter, or it doesn't want anyone to leave."

He had never, and would never, voice this opinion to the city leaders, but he had always been against building the walls. He thought of it as an eyesore to, what used to be, a beautiful little city. Now, the quaint and tranquil feeling he used to get when he looked upon the city in which he had grown up had been replaced by a foreboding harshness that made him feel uneasy. The world was changing quickly, and he would have to either keep up or be run over by it. He took a deep breath and pushed those feelings aside. There was nothing he could do about it today.

Tamari and Julis were soaking up the scenery as they rode through the city streets. They didn't come to Urna often but loved to see the busy people running to and fro through the city and smell the cakes sold by the vendors on the corners. Tamari would look wide-eyed at one spectacle only to be drawn away by another that Julis would point out to her. It was all exhilarating for a couple of farm girls from the countryside.

The carriage eventually pulled up beside what looked to be the largest house they had ever seen. There was a wall around the house's perimeter with gates spaced along the walls every thirty cubits. Within the gates were courtyards that filled the space between the walls and the house. Some of the courtyards were covered, while others were open. All were filled with flowers of all types and elaborately carved benches and reclining beds with soft pillowed coverings. There were servants at every turn, scurrying around, attending to all the flowers, and keeping everything immaculate. One was approaching the carriage to help Naamah down from her seat.

Tamari had seen this type of service very recently and suddenly knew where they were, "Father, this is Leader Bertlaw's house, isn't it?"

Hearing the unwelcoming tone in his daughter's voice, he reluctantly answered, "Yes, Tamari, it is. He invited us to come and visit them today." Jaylon braced himself for the reaction he thought would surely come but was surprised when it didn't.

Tamari wasn't happy about what she was being forced to endure, but she was becoming numb to it somehow. It even surprised her when she didn't react to the fact that she was being forced to spend another day with the last person she wanted to be nearby. She hated what her parents were trying to do and was determined it would not work. She resigned herself to getting through with the day's activities, whatever they were, but would not turn her back on the only person who was, at least lately, treating her with any respect; Methuselah. She didn't care how hard her parents pushed her toward this toad, Rimlah. She loved Methuselah, and that was all there was to it.

She stubbornly got down from the carriage on the opposite side of Julis, who was now being helped down by the servant. She then came around to within about five cubits of where her parents were. She stood expressionless as her mother derisively looked at her and rolled her eyes. Her father came over beside her and spoke softly, "I know you don't like this, but it would please your mother and me if you could be gracious to our hosts. We are guests here today. Can you please do that for me?"

He asked this so apologetically that Tamari was forced to relent. She solemnly nodded and joined the rest of the family.

The servant went to the nearest gate and rather properly turned on his heels and stood with his back arched while he announced their arrival. "The family of Jaylon has graciously come to the home of Leader Bertlaw, and I, your humble servant, Oresious, shall be honored to serve you in any way I can during your stay. Please follow me, honored guests." With this, he bowed slightly and waved his hand toward the entrance.

The family exchanged glances with each other and followed the servant's prompting. They hadn't expected such a formal greeting from the street. Oresious seemed to take great pride in his duty and was well suited for it. He was very well-dressed and very well-spoken. He was a bit rotund but wore it well, with a bright smile that made him almost instantly likable.

They walked single file through the outer courtyard, through a grand colonnade, and into an impressively decorated receiving room adorned with finely carved couches and flowers of all types and colors. On the walls were murals depicting beautiful scenes of the countryside. Tamari thought the big one in the center of the largest wall looked like the small valley in which Methuselah's family lived. It had a river with various wildlife, flowers, and trees beside it. There were birds, orchids, horses, turtles, and a behemoth that was feeding from the lower limbs of the stately cypress trees. The painting was beautifully done by what must have been the hand of a master artist. Tamari had never seen such workmanship as was displayed around the room.

Large bronze swords were also on the wall, crossed at the blades over highly polished shields. Tamari thought they were a bit out of place in the same room with these natural scenes of beauty; however, they were still very impressive.

Oresious excused himself and left the room only to return moments later. He again stood with his back arched and spoke in that same proper voice, "Family of Jaylon, I present your most gracious hosts, Leader Bertlaw and family." He said this with a flourish as he turned and backed away beside the doorway, bowing slightly and rolling his hand toward the opening.

Bertlaw, Zillah, and Rimlah filed in and stopped beside each other in such a way that showed they had done this many times before. They were all dressed in a very formal way, although a bit gaudily. Bertlaw wore a tri-colored tunic with a sizeable bejeweled gold chain. Zillah wore a tunic that was so brightly colored that it almost made one squint as they looked at her. She wore oversized earrings, rings, and a necklace that must have been a burden to carry. Rimlah similarly wore a tunic that had brightly colored flowers that could only be outdone next to what his mother was wearing. Tamari almost laughed out loud at the sight of these three hideously dressed souls. She held back all but an overly large smile that seemed to catch the eye of an obviously embarrassed Rimlah, though it was hard to notice his red face next to the tunic he wore.

"Welcome to our home, Jaylon. We are happy to have you here today," said Bertlaw. "Welcome to your beautiful family also. It is good to see you all again. Come with us into the dining hall. Our servants have prepared a very nice lunch for us today."

Bertlaw and his family turned in unison, headed back out the door through which they had come, and walked into the next room and down a hallway as Jaylon and his family followed. Each room they passed, as well as the hallway, was expansive and as elaborately decorated as the receiving room had been. There were identical swords, shields, and more murals, apparently done by the same expert hand.

Tamari thought that the artist must have spent years in this house to paint all these murals. She almost expected to see him in one of the rooms she passed, toiling away at another of his masterpieces. She thought of how she would like to meet the man responsible. He must be a fascinating person with a great depth of spirit. She would ask about him if she got the opportunity.

The procession finally ended when they entered a grand dining hall with a massive varnished wooden table filled with fruits and vegetables of every sort. This room also had murals and swords decorating the walls, along with lovely blue and yellow orchids on small shelved protrusions. There were large window openings half covered by ornately woven drapes. An expertly tended garden with large clamshell-shaped bird baths within a central courtyard could be seen through the windows. And everywhere one looked, a servant could be seen attending to the finest details of this stately and immaculate house. This place was awe-inspiring.

During the meal, polite small talk was made between the adults. Mostly, Naamah was admiring the things she wished she had for herself. She would look at Jaylon and say, "Jaylon, we should get one of those for our house," or, "Jaylon, you should have one built for me." Tamari just sat quietly and played with her food. She couldn't stand to hear her mother fawn over her snooty friends and their possessions this way and had eventually learned over the past few years to shut it out and get lost in her own thoughts.

She was suddenly jolted back to the present when her mother said her name, apparently for the second time, "Tamari, Rimlah asked you a question."

She recovered quickly, a bit embarrassed, "Oh, I'm sorry. I was lost in thought about something and didn't hear you. What was it you asked me?"

Rimlah was a little red in the face for having to ask the uncomfortable question again, only this time, with everyone watching intently. "I asked…uh… would you like to go for a carriage ride with me through Father's property down by the lakeside?"

Tamari didn't expect that question. If someone had said the sun was purple, she wouldn't have been caught more off guard, "Uh… I uh… don't know." She looked at her mother and saw the self-satisfied expression on her face, "Uh…" She looked at her father, who had an apologetic expression. "Uh… well…" she had to think quickly. "I don't know if I should. It's a long way, and I need to get back home with my parents…and, uh…"

Naamah broke in, "Don't be silly, Tamari. I'm sure that Rimlah will see to it that you are returned safely home after your ride. Wouldn't you, Rimlah?"

"Oh, of course. That would be no problem," Rimlah retorted, bright-eyed.

"But, Mother…" Tamari said before she was cut off.

"Then it is settled," said Bertlaw, lightly clapping his hands. "Rimlah and Tamari will take the carriage down through my property. Tamari, you will love it. That is one of the most beautiful places anywhere around. Jaylon, do not worry about her safety. I'll send Oresious, my most faithful and trustworthy servant, with them to ensure her safe return home."

Tamari felt trapped. She wanted no part in this but seemingly had no choice. She would have to spend more time with the person she most despised in this world. Not only that but now she had to be alone with him, with nowhere to run and nowhere to hide. Her only consolation was that Oresious would be there also. She hoped that he was as kind and likable as his smile let on.

Chapter 11

ENOCH HAD WALKED ALL THE PREVIOUS DAY AND MOST OF THE night, only stopping long enough to rest his feet and eat some bread from home and fruit he found along the river bank. It was now early afternoon, and he stopped to remove his sandals and soak his feet in the cool water. He sat on a large, flat rock, lay down, and closed his eyes as his feet dangled in the river. He had found a fig tree along the way and picked some off. Now, he was snacking on them while he rested his eyes from the bright sun.

He wanted to drift off to sleep for a while, but when he thought about how urgent the Lord had sounded about this mission of his, he would be jolted back to consciousness. However, he was starting to get blisters on his feet and had to stop and soak them before moving on. They would only get worse if he didn't stop and take care of them now.

Blisters weren't a new problem for Enoch. He had gotten several before while on his walks through the wilds and had learned to take ointments with him. But, before he could apply that ointment, he needed to soak his feet and soften the skin.

This resting and soaking of his feet had actually become one of his favorite parts of the walks. He would use this time to lay there and just soak in the solitude of nature. He loved to listen to the simple sounds of the river flowing, the birds singing, the frogs croaking, and the wind blowing through the leaves of the grass and trees. It was at least as therapeutic for him as was the ointment, if not more so. He would use this quiet time to contemplate his life and all the ways the Creator had blessed him. He felt he could hear the Creator's voice through the symphony of the natural world. And, he would pray.

As he lay there enjoying the soothing waters, he heard a noise. It sounded as if it came from the other side of the river. Then he heard it again, only a bit louder. It was a crunching sound, like plants being trampled by something very large and very heavy. Enoch sat up and surveyed his surroundings. He looked to the right, then to the left. Not seeing anything, he turned his head to scan the area again when something caught his eye in the tall grass down the same side of the riverbank he was on. It was very well camouflaged and hard to see. In fact, one second, it was there; the next, it was gone again, blending into the background.

Then, pushing through the grass into plain view, he saw it. It was an enormous male lion. He stood about three and a half cubits tall from the ground to his head and had a very dark brown mane that contrasted greatly with his bronze-colored hide. The lion's paws were huge and left heavy imprints about twice as big as Enoch's hands in the sand of the riverbank.

"Crunch," he heard the sound from the other side of the river again, this time closer. The lion kept moving toward him as he heard a low, guttural growl coming from the intimidating and beautiful beast. "Crunch" came again from the opposite bank. Enoch had never feared lions before since they only ate grasses and vegetables. Still, he had also never had one as intently focused on him as this one. Besides, this one was as large as he had ever seen. He was obviously very powerful, judging from the muscles that rippled under his short fur as he walked. "CRUNCH" from the opposite bank again, louder than ever.

Enoch wasn't sure where to look. The lion kept coming straight for him while the loud crunching was doing the same from the other side of the river. He did the only thing he knew to do in these types of situations; he said a quick, silent prayer for guidance.

The lion was only a few cubits away now and didn't seem to be slowing down or turning to the side. He just kept walking at the same steady pace. "CRUNCH!" This time, the ground shook. Then, the lion lifted his front paws from the ground and plopped them loudly and unceremoniously on the rock on either side of Enoch. Enoch froze.

The lion looked him right in the face and, to Enoch's surprise, purred and licked him as if the two of them were old friends. He didn't know what to do with his unbelievably sociable new friend. Finally, when he realized he wasn't doing so, Enoch started breathing again. "CRUNCH!!" the big cat just looked toward the noise, then looked back to Enoch and began licking him again. He couldn't understand why this lion wasn't at all concerned with what was obviously coming their way from across the river.

Enoch turned away from the friendly lion to wipe his face, which was now starting to chafe from the rough tongue of his new friend, and saw the head of an enormous behemoth coming into view over the tree line across the river. Once again, he wasn't particularly afraid of these gentle giants, but it, like the lion, was headed straight for him. He wondered what he was doing to attract all this attention from these animals.

Then, as the creature broke through the tree line, he saw something he hadn't counted on seeing. On the back of this enormous creature was his giant friend, Gardan. Enoch thought it a strange sight indeed to see a man riding on the back of such a creature as if it were a horse; however, given the enormous size of this particular friend, it was somehow fitting.

The behemoth came to a stop, straddling the river, and lowered his head to the ground a few cubits away from where Enoch was now standing. Gardan expertly spun, slid down the creature's neck, and dismounted close to his head. Gardan landed on his feet with an earthshaking thud.

"Enoch, my old friend!" he said with a beaming smile. "I have found you exactly where I was told that I would. It is good to see you again." Then he walked over and knelt so he could endearingly put both hands around Enoch's shoulders. He then shook him lightly. Lightly to his standards, but Enoch thought he would be crushed by this enthusiastic embrace.

"Be easy, my powerful friend. I see you haven't lost your strength over the years," Enoch said as he struggled not to cry out in pain. "It is, indeed, good to see you again." Enoch quizzically cocked his head, "You said that you found me exactly where you were told I would be. Who told you I would be here? I only stopped here a very short while ago and only to rest my feet."

Gardan eyed him thoughtfully, "I had a most unusual dream, my friend. In it, a man in a white tunic with a golden and purple sash told me I was to meet you here at this very spot. He said that you needed my help and that my redemption would come through the task I was to complete with you." Gardan shook his head as he looked to the ground in deep thought. "I have never had a dream like this one before. I didn't understand what he meant by his words, but his eyes had great power. Those most unusual eyes also held within them a love that made me feel as if I were important to him. My friend, I have never seen such love in the eyes of anyone. You have a great kindness in your eyes, but nothing like this." Then, he looked at Enoch. "You know this man, do you not? Was this the Lord you spoke to me about so many years ago?"

"Yes," Enoch said with a tear in his eye. "Yes, my friend. He is the Creator I spoke of. What He told you is true. He came to me also and told me to seek you out. I don't know exactly what it is that we are to do yet, but He said I would need your help." A look of concern crossed Enoch's face, "I only know that my future daughter-in-law is in great danger and that we must hurry back to help her."

Gardan stood again, towering over Enoch at three times his height, "Then let us not waste any more time." He then turned and patted the head of the lion. "I see you have already met Leeno here. He has been a most loyal companion to me in my solitude here in this wilderness." He then walked over to the behemoth, which was now eating the lush greenery along the river. "And this little lady is Nahla. I rescued her from a bog she fell into a few years ago, and since then, she has never left my side."

Enoch was patting Leeno and scratching his head under his ears, causing him to purr loudly. He then walked over to Nahla and rubbed her neck, eliciting a reverberating purr. Enoch laughed. "I am pleased to meet you both. One can never have too many friends of your size."

With that, Gardan said, "Nahla, up!" The colossal creature turned and swung its tail around to where they were standing. Leeno nonchalantly hopped the tree-like tail as it swung by, as if he had done it many times before. Then Gardan reached around Enoch's back and under his arms with his giant palm covering his whole chest, picked him up as if he weighed nothing, and walked onto the creature's tail. Nahla gently raised her tail so they could walk easily down it and onto her back. Gardan sat Enoch down in front of him and took up position behind. He then grabbed a rope fashioned around Nahla's neck like a stirrup and tugged it toward the north. She gently turned and started walking. Enoch was amazed at how smooth the ride was.

"This is quite a view from up here," Enoch said with a wide-eyed expression.

Gardan laughed heartily, "It's faster than walking and easier on the feet."

Enoch agreed, thinking about the blisters forming on his feet before Gardan found him by the river. He smiled and thought of how much he loved the Lord for his mercy. The Creator had even had compassion on his feet. He prayed a thankful prayer and settled in for the long ride.

Tamari and Rimlah rode silently along the road toward the west and Bertlaw's property while Oresious drove the carriage, whistling a happy little tune. She couldn't help but feel betrayed by her parents for making her go on this little foray with, of all people, Rimlah. She was determined not to talk to him. She was going to make him feel as lonely as she was feeling. Perhaps, if she treated him as if he weren't there, he would take the hint and give up on his pointless pursuit of a relationship that would not happen. She would just ride along, looking out the small window in the carriage.

"Tamari, I'm sorry for the way this came about." Rimlah got no response. He searched for something to say that would put her at ease. "I realize that you don't like me. I can't say that I blame you. I haven't treated you or Methuselah very well. I guess I was just jealous. There just aren't many girls as nice as you in Urna, and…"

Tamari abruptly interrupted, "Well, if you like me so much, why do you act like such a hateful idiot toward me?" She didn't mean to say anything. It just came out before she realized it.

Rimlah gave it a moment before he spoke again, "As I said, I'm sorry. Really, I am. I promise not to act that way toward you anymore."

He sounded so sincere in how he said it that it caught her off guard. Tamari was never very good at holding grudges, and she could feel her defenses falling away. However, she continued looking out the window without acknowledging him.

"Tamari, it wasn't my idea to drag you out here this way. My parents, and I suspect yours too, have decided to push us together. I told them that you didn't like me, but they insisted that, after we spent some time together, you would warm up to me." Rimlah waited to see if that got any response.

Tamari was somewhat surprised at his statement and reluctantly turned and eyed him suspiciously. "You mean to tell me that this was our *parent's* idea? You weren't the one pushing for this?"

Rimlah shifted in his seat to face her, "Yes. Like I said, I told them it wouldn't work, that you weren't interested in me that way, but they insisted. *I* didn't even have a choice. I would rather not be here right now either." Then, realizing how that probably sounded, he tried to clarify his remark, "Not that I wouldn't enjoy your company, but not if it was against your will. Even a *'hateful idiot'* like me wouldn't want to force you to do anything against your wishes."

She smiled at his play on her own words. "It *won't* work, you know. Our parent's little scheme to get us together, I mean. I love *Methuselah*. Their meddling will not change that."

"I know," said Rimlah, a bit despondently. "I can see that. I would, however, like to be friends. Do you think you could give me another chance if I promise to treat you, and even Methuselah, better in the future?"

Tamari eyed him for any sign of guile but saw only sincerity in his words. She turned and looked back out the little window for a moment before turning around and answering, "*If* you promise to act like a friend instead of acting like a goon the way you do with your stupid friends, I think I could give you another chance. But you also have to apologize to Methuselah. You have never been anything but hateful to him, and you must convince *him* of your sincerity too."

Rimlah took a deep breath and answered, "Alright; I don't know if he will be as forgiving as you, but I will apologize to him."

Tamari smiled, "I think you will find him to be more gracious than you think. He really *is* a very nice person."

Rimlah smiled broadly, "I will go to his house tomorrow, and I will speak to him." He took a deep breath of relief. "You know, I'm sorry it had to happen this way, but I am glad that we were able to resolve this situation. I need more good friends. I wouldn't call the friends I have 'good' ones."

"Neither would I, Rimlah. You know, people judge you by the company you keep. I believe, deep down, you are nothing like them. Why do you spend any time with them?" Tamari asked.

Rimlah thought for a moment, "I suppose, it's because their parents are on the council with my father. He says that I should be around people of our station in life. I guess, just like today, I didn't have much choice in the matter."

Tamari looked at him thoughtfully, "What will they say about your being friends with me and Methuselah then?"

Rimlah thought for a moment, "Well, they won't have a problem with *you* because of your father's emerald mines, but Methuselah is a different story altogether. The people of the city think his father is a bit strange, to say the least."

Tamari answered quickly and passionately, "Rimlah, I have known his family for my whole life. They are the nicest, most giving people I have ever met. I know what you mean though. My father feels the same way, but if you talk to Enoch, there is wisdom in what he says. He is also a very sweet and gentle man. I look forward to, one day, being his daughter-in-law. I love him and his wife as if they were my own parents, and I'm sure, if you get to know them, you would feel the same way."

Rimlah smiled and nodded, "Then, that is what I will have to do."

For the rest of the ride, they spoke of lighter subjects, just trying to get to know each other in a way they could never have before. It turned out, Tamari thought to herself, that Rimlah was a lot more likable than she thought.

The small, quiet farming village of Pargo was nestled amidst the low hills that surrounded a small creek, which flowed serenely through the prairies to the southeast of the land of Nod. The people of Pargo were few in number but self-sufficient. They were separated from the other towns by a great distance. The residents were a group of people who chose to leave the larger cities of Nod to live a simpler life outside of the increasingly violent societies that inhabited their former homes. There were no walls or soldiers with swords and shields to threaten their safety.

The armies of those cities had become a hindrance to the people. Instead of buying what they needed, they had become more of a criminal enterprise, demanding what they wanted. The soldiers would order the people to give them supplies in return for their protection. However, if one did not give in to their demands, those same soldiers would just take what they wanted and destroy the lives of the very people they were supposed to protect.

Having had enough of being frightened by these so-called protectors, some of the farmers and artisans of those cities banded together to form villages like Pargo. Here, they were free to live their lives in peace and harmony. They could raise their children and grow their crops free from the worries of city life. They were, once again, happy and flourishing.

The village of Pargo was enjoying a beautiful day in the mid-morning sun. The farmers were tending their fields while the smell of baking bread wafted through the small valley. Little did they suspect what evils were coming their way.

Skaldan and Syclah had been walking for two days through the dry terrain of the southwest corner of Nod. They were hungry, thirsty, and in a foul mood.

Their father, Azazel, had sent them out to wreak havoc among the cities that had resisted his offers of services. He had tried to sell them on the need to protect themselves from each other. Still, some of them insisted that they had no need for it since they had never been threatened by anything before. He was now determined to show them what they needed protection from.

As the two giant men reached the top of a rise, they could smell the aroma of baking bread. Their stomachs growled in anticipation of something to eat. Skaldan looked over at his freakish brother and smiled. "It seems that we have found our next meal, Brother."

Syclah grunted indecipherably as he picked up the pace toward the next rise in the pasturelands. Atop this hill, they spotted their target. A sleepy little village below with no walls to protect it lay unsuspectingly below him. The two looked at each other and smiled maliciously before they descended toward their quarry.

A short time later, the two sat by the creek eating the loaves of bread and cakes they had gathered from among the wreckage of homes. All around them lay the broken and mutilated bodies of all who dared to be around when their devastating rage had begun. After devouring their spoils and drinking all the water they wanted from the creek, they rose and headed further east.

There was another place to visit where some of the people had resisted the services of their father. The people of this city had ultimately decided to go along. Still, their progress was slow, and Azazel felt they needed a reminder of what could happen if they dragged their feet for too long.

Besides that, there was also a man in this city who had taught the people of the area how to read and write. He was said to have gotten this knowledge directly from the Creator Himself. This man would have to be made an example of. Azazel was very specific about this. He would not have this man teaching people the words of God, the eternal enemy of Azazel's master. This man, Enoch, would pay for his deeds.

Chapter 12

THE LAKE WAS SERENE AND PLACID AS THE MIDDAY SUN STOOD above. The gentle breeze pushed tiny waves along the surface as the ethereal mists rode effortlessly overhead. The lakeshore was lined with fruit trees and flowers of all varieties and colors alongside the reeds and grasses. All around the lake was an abundance of wildlife in wide varieties and colors as the flowers. Giant black and white swans were regally floating near the shore as hummingbirds darted from bloom to bloom feeding on the sweet nectar of the trumpet-shaped flowers. In the distance were two twenty-cubit-long horned and spike-tailed lizards lazily lying on the bank, the sun glinting off the large scales protruding upright from their backs. Further in the distance, distorted slightly by the ghostly mists, were a group of behemoths reaching up into the branches of the large trees feeding on the tender green leaves. Their wraithlike calls could be heard from across the lake as if moaning thunder erupted from the depths of their bellies.

Tamari and Rimlah, having finished their lunch, were reclining on the wooden couches that adorned the small pier extending out into the lake. Having had extensive conversations on various subjects while eating their meal, they now lay quietly, taking in the beauty of this place. Tamari thought this might be one of the most picturesque places she had ever seen. Rimlah's father had, indeed, told the truth about it. This thought reminded her of something she was curious about.

"Rimlah," she said as she sat up and faced him, "I wanted to ask you. Who painted the murals on the walls of your parent's home? I don't think I have ever seen such skilled artwork before."

Rimlah turned a little red in the face and smiled at her sheepishly, "Would you believe, I painted them?"

Tamari gave him an incredulous look, "Rimlah, really, who painted them? I *really* want to know."

"Tamari, I really *did* paint them myself. I know that I haven't been too trustworthy in the past, but I really did paint them," he said as he sat up and faced her squarely.

Tamari gazed thoughtfully at him for a moment before asking her next question. "Then, how did you learn to paint that way? And why doesn't anyone know about it? If you painted those murals, you're obviously very talented. You should let people know about it. Then people could see a whole other side of your personality."

"You don't understand, Tamari. It's not that I don't want people to see my artwork." He took a deep breath before continuing, "You see, when I was about eight years old, I liked to draw and sketch things like animals and trees, even people, but my parents saw it as a waste of time. My father always wanted me to learn how to make money. My mother always wanted me to learn about the social graces. She taught me how to treat people more important than us and climb higher on the social ladder. Then, she also taught me how to treat people she deemed to be lower on the social ladder." With this, he looked down momentarily before looking back at her apologetically. "I guess you've already seen the evidence of my aptitude for that. Once again, I'm truly sorry." Rimlah paused again to give weight to his apology.

Tamari waved her hand as if she were swatting that thought away. "I told you, Rimlah, as long as you stop acting like that, it will be forgotten. Now, please continue. What you're telling me still doesn't explain why your parents don't want your talents to be revealed to the world."

"Well, I guess they just think it's beneath me to be a lowly artist. They would rather me learn and continue the family business. They didn't want me to paint at all for the longest time, but I have this unexplainable need to paint sometimes that seems to take me over. So, I made them a deal; if they would allow me to paint the murals that you saw in the house, then I would learn my father's business. Also, as a stipulation, I wouldn't tell anyone about my painting. So, I'm afraid I'm going to have to ask you not to tell anyone what I just told you. It could prove to be quite embarrassing to my parents."

Tamari looked at him incredulously, "You mean that I can't tell anyone *at all* about your painting? You have this amazing gift from God, and I have to keep it a *secret*?"

"I would appreciate it if you would, yes," Rimlah said with pleading in his eyes.

Tamari gazed toward the ground, lightly shaking her head. "It doesn't make sense to me why your parents want to keep it such a secret, but you can trust me if that is what you want. No one will hear it from me. I promise." Still shaking her head, she continued half under her breath, "If my son could paint like that, I would be so proud that I would tell *everyone*."

"Thank you, Tamari," Rimlah said with a diluted smile. "I appreciate it. You know, you're the only person outside of our household to know about that. It feels good to finally be able to tell someone about something that seems to be such a large part of me. It's kind of freeing."

"I'm glad I got the chance to learn more about you than what you projected before," Tamari said. "It's funny. You've gone from being one of my least favorite people to one of my most favorite people within half a day." Then, she looked earnestly at him,

"Rimlah, please don't betray my newfound trust in you. I promise I won't be as forgiving as this if you do."

Rimlah held his hand up in oath to his new friend, "I promise."

The two went back to relaxing and enjoying the beautiful scenery again. Rimlah couldn't help but smile both outside and within himself. He had always had such a crush on this new friend but now saw her in a whole new light. He still adored her and thought she was the most beautiful girl he had ever seen, but his feelings for her had somehow changed. Instead of being someone he wanted to impress and capture as his own, she was now a trusted friend and someone he didn't want to disappoint. He understood that she would probably never be his, but she would always be his friend. In fact, she was perhaps the first real friend he ever had. The pure satisfaction of that fact was a new feeling that washed over him in a cascade of contentment he had never known.

The quiet of the moment was interrupted by a sound in the distance. The noise was hard to place, but as Rimlah and Tamari both looked toward the disturbance's direction, they sensed a foreboding in their spirits about it.

Oresious had been reclining under a tree near the carriage. He, too, felt the change in the atmosphere and came immediately to his feet. He stood and gazed intently toward the direction of the disturbance for a moment. Down the shore, he saw the birds take flight in a scattershot fashion as if fleeing for safety. Then, through the mist, he saw the silhouettes of two gigantic creatures. He thought for a moment that the behemoths were making their way around the lake, but their shapes weren't quite right. Then, as the two figures became clearer, Oresious ran for the carriage and called for his two charges.

"Rimlah! Tamari! We must go now!" Oresious yelled as he reached the carriage, pulled a large gleaming bronze sword from beneath the driver's seat, and stood with it at the ready between the carriage and the approaching giants.

Tamari and Rimlah stood and kept staring at the two large figures. They were moving closer at a surprising pace for their steady and effortless strides.

"What is it, Oresious?" yelled Rimlah as they began walking toward the carriage without taking their eyes off the new arrivals.

Oresious, clearly annoyed with their lack of concern, barked back at them, "Now! Get yourselves on the carriage now!"

Rimlah's eyes grew wide with fear as he now could see clearly what Oresious was so worried about. The two shapes were actually the two largest men he had ever seen, and they were dressed for battle. He grabbed Tamari by the hand and almost dragged her toward the carriage, jolting her out of shock. Finally, reaching the carriage, Rimlah threw her into the back and climbed on himself. Having them both aboard, Oresious vaulted into the driver's seat and grabbed the reins. The cart was facing the oncoming warriors and needed to be turned around. Oresious slapped the reins and yelled, "*Yah, Yah!*" The horses, who also seemed shocked at the sight of the giant men, finally came to life and jumped into a full gallop as they started the wide arc to turn toward safety and away from danger.

Just as the carriage was nearly broadside to the approaching giants, the larger of the two, who had only one eye, took a quick step and bounded the gap of thirty cubits toward the escapees while pulling his massive sword from its scabbard. He swiped down and cut the horses cleanly in half in one lightning-fast motion. The horses let out a short, unearthly squeal as they drenched the ground with their blood. The carriage's momentum caused it to lurch awkwardly over the severed carcasses, throwing its occupants to the ground beyond.

Rimlah and Tamari landed inelegantly and lay stunned on the ground, but Oresious, as if he had been trained for just such an occasion, rolled gracefully back to his feet and positioned himself between the two teens and their attackers.

"Rimlah, take Tamari and run! Run as fast as you can! Don't take time to look back! Run!" said Oresious as he gallantly stood in the gap.

Rimlah grabbed Tamari's hand and jerked her to her feet. "No Oresious, I won't..."

Without turning to look at him, Oresious snapped back. "Do as you are told, Boy! Run!"

With that, Rimlah turned and ran as fast as he could, dragging Tamari behind.

Oresious stood his ground fearlessly and with some malice in his eyes. "Those were my two favorite horses you killed, you ugly beast! I'm afraid I'll have to punish you for that," he said, looking the giant in his one freakish eye.

Syclah stood blinking, amazed at the bravery with which this little man was standing up to him. Finally, his amazement gave way to anger as he raised his sword to dispatch this tiny warrior. As he started to swing toward his target, Oresious, with surprising speed, rolled beneath his legs and expertly cut the tendon behind the ankle of the giant's left leg, causing Syclah to wail loudly in pain and stumble forward to one knee. Oresious rolled away from the second giant, who was now approaching and drawing his own sword.

Skaldan eyed his tiny foe with astonishment. He glanced back to his brother, who was now nursing his lower leg and whimpering. "You are fairly skilled with that sword. I am impressed, but you have only outwitted an idiot. You won't find me so easy to outsmart."

Oresious grinned slightly to hide the fear that was welling up inside of him. "I should warn you that I have trained with the best swordsmen in Urna."

"That may be," said Skaldan. "But my father, Azazel, taught them all."

Oresious instantly recognized the name. Azazel had been the one who sold the city leaders on the idea of raising an army.

Oresious now understood better where the evil he faced had come from. "Your father's business in Urna is complete. What does he want from these good people now?"

Skaldan circled his quarry with intense eyes. "You have one among you named Enoch who says he speaks with the Creator. He speaks against my father's master and must be dealt with."

"Enoch?" This indeed surprised Oresious. "Enoch is a man of peace. He is a good man. He has only spoken out against the evil that men have done toward each other. Who is the master of Azazel that he would want to do harm to Enoch?"

Skaldan smiled derisively at Oresious and answered maliciously, "My father's master is the one true god, the father of evil himself." With that, he lunged toward Oresious with a full-frontal attack, swinging his sword in circling arcs and driving Oresious backward.

When Skaldan had swung his sword around himself and was somewhat off balance, Oresious sprang in the opposite direction, ran past him, and sliced Skaldan deeply along the lower thigh before he realized what had happened.

Skaldan turned and took an awkward slice backward at him. When his full weight came down on the injured leg, he finally felt the searing pain and grabbed at his leg. He then pulled his hand up and eyed the blood. His eyes burned with anger, and again attacked with the same result on the calf of his lower leg on the opposite side. Skaldan howled in rage.

Realizing that the little man's speed would be a difficult problem to overcome, Skaldan looked over at his brother, who was still sitting on the ground, nursing his ankle. His brother caught his eyes and followed them as Skaldan silently directed him toward a large stone beside him. Skaldan then circled around so as to put Oresious' back toward Syclah.

Oresious hadn't noticed the silent exchange between the two. Understandably, his complete attention had been on the sword of the giant man intent on taking his life. As Skaldan began swinging his sword again to signal another frontal assault, Oresious was blindsided by the weight of the enormous stone as it crashed into his back, throwing him and his sword to the ground in opposite directions.

Oresious tried to get up, but his legs didn't respond. He was paralyzed and could only watch as Skaldan walked over and stood above him, smiling an evil grin down on him. "You fought bravely but, as I told you; you won't be able to outsmart me so easily."

Oresious looked up at the hulking figure and winced in pain. "I am only one little man with a sword, and you almost got bested by me. What do you think you can do to a man like Enoch who has the Lord, Creator of all, on his side? You have already lost." With that, Oresious couldn't help but smile up at his executioner.

This comment cut deeply into the mind of the massive warrior. With one final howl of anger, Skaldan brought his sword down, splitting the brave Oresious lengthwise.

Chapter 13

Rimlah and Tamari ran as fast as they could. Behind them, over their footfalls and heavy breathing, Rimlah heard the clashing of swords a few times. He could only think of how brave Oresious had been to stay behind and fend off the strange giant attackers that had come out of nowhere. "Who were they?" he thought to himself. "Why did they assail us that way without any provocation?" Then he heard a faint cry of pain from their rear. They were some distance away now, but Rimlah knew this painful shriek didn't come from Oresious. He stopped running to listen more intently.

Tamari was surprised at the sudden stop and wheeled around at the end of his arm due to her momentum. She watched Rimlah's face as he turned to face back toward the direction from which they had come. Sensing she was about to say something, he held up his hand and leaned into his ear. After a few moments of silence, he finally offered a quick explanation, "That cry of pain didn't come from Oresious. I think that was one of those giants."

Tamari looked at him in astonishment. "But… those men were so big and powerful! How could Oresious have hurt one of *them*?" She whispered this, knowing Rimlah was still trying to hear what he could.

Answering in the same hushed tone, he replied, "Oresious is probably the finest swordsman in the army of Urna. It will take more than size and power to defeat him."

They stood silently for a moment before hearing a different scream. This one came from someone else. Rimlah looked at Tamari and gave a reassuring nod, "I believe that was the second assailant meeting with his end. As I said, Oresious, despite appearances, isn't a man to be trifled with."

With that, Rimlah grabbed her by the hand and started back toward the direction of those pained screams. Tamari was surprised by his actions and stopped him. "Where are you going?" she said with a look of incredulity.

"We should go back to see if Oresious is alright. I am sure he made short work of those two," Rimlah answered confidently.

Tamari shook her head. "I don't feel good about it. I think we should keep going."

Rimlah contemplated this for a moment before replying, "Alright, we can wait here for a few minutes. I'm sure Oresious will be along soon."

Tamari eyed him quizzically for a moment. She was a bit surprised at his cavalier attitude toward the whole situation, "Don't you feel that we should, at least, hide where we can see whether it's Oresious or one of those hideous giants who comes? I would hate to be exposed and out in the open if you're wrong."

Rimlah nodded his approval, "We can hide if it will make you feel better."

They looked around them momentarily before Rimlah spotted a large rock about twenty cubits off the main path. "There is a good place. We should be able to see who is coming by from behind there."

The two of them settled in behind the large rock. From their vantage point, they couldn't see the road behind them very well, but they could see anyone approaching until they passed. Tamari gave her approval, "Thank you, Rimlah. I hope you are right about Oresious, but there's no harm in being cautious."

"You're right, Tamari. There *is* no harm in being cautious." Rimlah let a few silent moments pass before speaking again, "I wonder what those two wanted back there anyway. And why did they attack us like that without any provocation? It doesn't make any sense to me. What did *we* do to cause them to attack us?"

"I don't know," said Tamari, whispering in an attempt at relaying the hint to Rimlah that they should be quiet until the danger had passed.

"I mean to cut down our horses that way…" continued Rimlah at the same conversational volume he started with.

"Shhhh!" said Tamari. "We need to be quiet. Besides, I think I heard something."

With Rimlah finally quiet, they listened.

"Drrrag, thud. Drrrag, thud. Drrrag, thud."

Tamari and Rimlah just looked at each other in bewilderment. Both sets of eyes asked the same question. "What was that?" The sound was definitely coming down the road. The only solace was that they would both know exactly what it was in a moment when it passed by.

"Drrrag, thud. Drrrag, thud. Drrrag, thud." It was going by now. "Drrrag, thud. Drrrag, thud."

Then they saw him. It was the giant with the one freakish eye dragging a lame foot behind him. Rimlah and Tamari gave each other a startled and fearful look. Besides that, they were now in this hideous creature's line of sight if it were to turn around in their direction. Rimlah slowly and quietly grabbed Tamari's hand and motioned that they should ease their way around to the back side of the rock.

They backed their way gingerly around as silently as possible while keeping their eyes on the injured giant. They finally made it around and out of sight. They closed their eyes, took a silent deep breath, and turned to lean their backs against the rock.

Before opening her eyes, Tamari heard the sound of rushing wind. She opened them just in time to hear the dull, bone-crushing impact and to see Rimlah disappear from her peripheral vision. When she turned to see what had happened, she only saw him collide head-first into the base of a large tree about fifteen cubits away and fall limp to the ground the way only a dead man would.

Wide-eyed and frozen in terror, she slowly turned back to the source of the mayhem. There in front of her was the biggest man she had ever seen. He was bent at the waist and looking directly down into her face.

With rancid breath, he spoke in an evil tone, "You're a pretty thing, aren't you? I think I'll keep you for myself. While my brother heals, I'll have something to play with." This caused Skaldan to unleash an eerie, malicious cackle.

Her senses were overloaded, her knees buckled, and blackness fell over Tamari.

Methuselah and Jubal were unusually quiet as they sat on the bank of the river that passed through Enoch's valley. The birds sang loudly as they flitted and flew around them, playing their little version of a "catch me if you can" game. Off in the distance, the behemoths were bellowing to each other in their own secret language that could be heard over great distances. But Methuselah could only hear the thoughts in his head echoing the same unanswerable questions he had been asking for the last three days. "Why did Dolan do that to me? Why did he lure me in front of Tamari's family and embarrass me like that? Who were all those people that were laughing at me?" Those questions were nagging him greatly, but the question that bothered him the most was the one that rang loudest in his ears. "Why was Tamari dressed so nicely and standing next to Rimlah?"

Then, there was something new that was bothering him. He had the urge to pray for them both, Tamari *and* Rimlah. He had awakened with that thought foremost in his mind early that morning, and he couldn't seem to shake it. He wanted to pray for Rimlah about as much as he wanted to drown himself. He couldn't stand even the thought of it, but the urge just *would not* go away.

"I wonder what they are saying to each other," said Jubal, jarring Methuselah out of his thoughts.

With a slight shake of his head, Methuselah looked at him inquisitively. "What?"

"The behemoths, I wonder what they are saying to each other," answered Jubal.

"I have no idea," said Methuselah. Then, with a wry smirk and his best behemoth voice, he added, "They are probably telling each other, 'Don't trust the female behemoths!'." They both laughed deeply. For Methuselah, this was his first real laugh in three days, and it felt good to him.

After a few more giggles between them, it got quiet again for a while before Methuselah finally decided to share with Jubal what he was thinking, "Jubal, I woke up this morning with a strange urge to pray for Tamari and, believe it or not, Rimlah. I know it sounds crazy, but I feel like I need to pray for them both."

Jubal stared at him wide-eyed briefly before replying, "I can understand praying for Tamari. She has to live with her mother and father. That alone deserves some prayer, but for *Rimlah* too?"

"Like I said, it sounds a little crazy, but I just can't shake it. I think I'm supposed to pray for them *both*," said Methuselah.

Jubal thought for a minute. "Did you tell your mother about this?"

"No, she's been acting worried enough about something. That was also strange, the way she was worried about the other people at that party. She asked if anyone was missing. That was an odd thing to ask, wasn't it?" asked Methuselah with a genuine look of confusion.

"Odd would be the right word alright." Jubal thought a moment, "When will your father be home?"

Methuselah gazed thoughtfully across the river. "I don't know exactly. That, in itself, isn't so odd, but I get the feeling that this wasn't one of his usual walks. Mother told me to stay around the house until he returned. Something is happening, but I'm at a loss to figure what it may be."

"Well," Jubal said with a deep breath. "I guess you'll find out soon enough. In the meantime, it sounds like you have some praying to do. Would you like some company or is it something you feel like you should do on your own?"

Methuselah smiled broadly at his cousin with an expression of great appreciation, "Thank you, Jubal. I would like that. Besides, two are always better than one."

With that, the two boys knelt and prayed fervently, as their fathers had taught them.

Chapter 14

RIMLAH FELT THE SENSATION OF MOVEMENT FOLLOWED BY an explosion of pain in his head and left shoulder. He opened his eyes but immediately shut them again as the brilliant light of day intruded into them and caused the pain to intensify in his head. He was dazed and thought he was caught somewhere between dream and reality. He could feel himself lying down on something soft while also feeling the rhythmic jarring of the road underneath him as he moved along the path.

Once again, he tried to open his eyes ever so slightly, learning quickly from his first attempt. His sight was hazy and unfocused. He heard the sound of moaning and struggled to make sense of it until it finally dawned on him that those sounds were actually coming from himself. This was followed by more flashes of searing pain, causing him to grip tightly the hand that had hold of his own.

"Quiet, dear boy," came the soothingly melodic voice of his apparent caretaker. "You are going to be alright. The Lord has great things in mind for you, Rimlah."

Rimlah was amazed at how the mere sound of this man's voice seemed to ease his pain. He tried once again to open his eyes. This time, his sight was a bit clearer. He squinted up at the face that was looking down at him. He saw the man's bright blue eyes framed by golden hair and the most beautiful skin he had ever seen. There also seemed to be a brilliant but soft light emanating from this man. The light seemed warm and soothing while somehow eliciting feelings of pure love. It was like nothing Rimlah had ever experienced. He thought to himself that he must be dreaming all of this.

Rimlah tried to form words, but they came out more like a croak from his dry throat. The golden-haired man gave him a drink of water while lovingly holding his head, which seemed not to hurt as much as before. Rimlah swallowed and tried again to speak. "Am I dead... or dreaming this?"

This brought a hearty chuckle from his mysterious caretaker and at least two others Rimlah hadn't noticed around him. "No, my friend. You are quite alive, I assure you. As I said, the Lord has great things in mind for you. You just rest now. Go back to sleep, and you will feel much better when you wake."

With that, the golden-haired man put his hand on his forehead. Immediately, Rimlah drifted back to a restful and contented sleep.

Azazel and his remaining three sons had left their fortress in the northwestern region of Nod. They set up an encampment in a heavily wooded area in the hills outside Urna. Here, he planned on waiting for Skaldan and Syclah to wreak their havoc upon Urna's surrounding villages and then bring to him the man, Enoch, who claimed to talk with the Creator.

The mere mention of his name infuriated Azazel. Enoch had been teaching people how to read and write the language of God so that they might know the will of their Creator and the purposes of their creation. Azazel saw this as an unfair intrusion on his master's domain. The Creator had cast Lucifer out of heaven and banished him and his followers to this world. If his master could not rule heaven, he would indeed rule this place, whether the Creator liked it or not. Now, the God of Heaven had the audacity to infringe on even this territory? As far as Azazel was concerned, this was blasphemous toward his master's assumed divinity and supreme authority. This man, Enoch, would have to have an example made of him.

He had been anxious for this moment for many years since he first heard of Enoch's sins against his master. Now, he would be able to exact the punishment for his transgressions. His pulse quickened when he heard Skaldan and Syclah coming up the wooded path toward the camp.

However, Azazel was quite disappointed when Skaldan came into view with the crying and squirming female draped over his shoulder, followed by a whimpering Syclah dragging a lame foot. His anger grew as he watched Skaldan come into camp and drop the girl to the forest floor with a thud, and without even glancing in his direction. Skaldan proceeded to tie his prize between two trees with her arms outstretched. The girl continued to squirm and fight against him until a look of terror came across her face when she finally noticed that she was now among not two but five giants. Securely fastened into place, she quietly stared in disbelief at her surroundings.

Azazel walked over with his arms behind his back and spoke in an almost guttural growl as he eyed the new visitor. "What is this? This is *not* what I asked for!"

Skaldan looked at him apologetically and attempted an answer, "Father, I..."

"And what happened to your oaf of a brother? Why is he limping so badly?" interrupted Azazel.

"Father, please listen to me. We were..."

"You were what!? I gave you specific instructions, but you bring me this girl instead? What possible reason could there be for this?" Azazel asked while looking at Skaldan now.

"Father, please let me answer!" Skaldan gave it a moment before he spoke again, expecting to be interrupted. He was surprised when no interruption came. He then told the whole story of how he came to have this girl. He continued, "Father, the little man asked me why we were here before I killed him, and I told him we were after the man, Enoch. He seemed to know him, so I thought that maybe the two that were with him might also know him. When this girl finally came to, I asked her. It would seem that she knows him well. Perhaps he knows her well enough that Enoch will probably be one of the men who will come looking for her."

Azazel gave this some thought for a moment before speaking, "But, how will he know where to find her?"

Skaldan's countenance brightened with this question, seeing an opportunity to return to his father's good graces. "That is where we were somewhat fortunate. Syclah's injury has left an easily followed track from there to here. Also, when they come for her, instead of having two of us to deal with, they will have five. We should easily be able to have our way with them. Then, you can make this man, Enoch, watch as you make examples out of them all, including this pretty young thing."

Azazel gave this some thoughtful consideration before a broad smile appeared on his face. "Skaldan, my son, perhaps you're not the idiot I thought you were."

When the old man in the gardener's cart pulled up to Bertlaw's house in Urna, the servants gasped at the sight of the load he was carrying. The strongest of the three servants quickly grabbed the sleeping form and whisked him straight into the house. The others asked the old man what had happened.

The kindly old gardener answered, "There was quite a mess out by the lakeside on Bertlaw's property. I'm sorry to say that this young man was the only one I found besides Oresious. It was too late for him I'm afraid, but Rimlah here is going to be alright. The Creator has seen fit to heal him. Tell Bertlaw to go get Jaylon and Enoch to help track down the girl. Tell him to start at first light tomorrow morning."

One of the servants turned and told the other to do as the old man said and give Bertlaw the message, then watched as he ran into the house. When he turned to face the old man again, there was nothing and no one there. Nor was there anything in either direction when he ran out into the street to see where he had gone. He then ran into the house to make his own report.

Bertlaw and Zillah were just finishing their evening meal when they heard the commotion from the receiving room of the house. They exchanged a curious glance before one of the servants called out frantically. "Master Bertlaw, come quickly! Master Bertlaw, Rimlah is injured!"

With this, they both shot up from the table. Zillah, in a manner that betrayed her elite status, brushed her husband out of the way and ran toward her injured son. When she entered the room, she saw him lying on one of the couches with dried blood all over his head, matting down his hair. He was lying so still and peacefully that it caused her to stop in her tracks and put her hands over her mouth to muffle the involuntary shriek of horror that came through.

Bertlaw now entered the room and, upon seeing the sight, took two steps and almost fell down while going to his knees to kneel beside his son. The second servant now entered and spoke up to cut their gruesome thoughts short, "Master Bertlaw, the man who brought him said he would be alright. He said that the Creator had healed him."

Bertlaw turned and gave the servant a disbelieving stare as the third servant entered from outside. "What do you mean, 'the Creator has healed him?' Can you not see all the blood? Get me a wash basin and some cloth to clean him up!" He looked back to his pitiful son and, with some difficulty, choked back his emotions. After a moment, he returned to the servant who had just entered the room. "Where is the man who brought him? I would like to ask him a few questions. And why didn't Oresious bring him? Where is *he*?"

The servant answered as best he could, measuring his words carefully, "Master Bertlaw, the man who brought Master Rimlah said that Oresious was dead." He thought he should pause there momentarily and let this disturbing news stand on its own before continuing. He knew how close the family, and for that matter, his fellow servants, had been to Oresious.

"Dead?" Bertlaw stared off, blinking toward an empty corner of the room. "How could he be dead?"

"The man did not say how he died except that there was what he called a 'mess' down by the lake." He paused again as the other servant returned with the wash basin and cloth, setting them down beside Bertlaw.

Zillah, now kneeling on the other side of the couch, motioned for her husband to give them to her as tears streamed down her face. Bertlaw watched intently as she lovingly and gently started to wash the blood out of her son's hair. She poured the cold water over his head and suddenly shrieked again when Rimlah opened his eyes and looked up at her. "He's alive!" she screamed excitedly. "He's alive!"

"M-Mother?" Rimlah muttered as though he were dreaming.

Bertlaw immediately stood up on his knees and looked into his son's open eyes, "Rimlah, my son, you are alive!" With the expression of a father who had looked upon his newborn son for the first time, his eyes danced around the room at all the servants before returning to Rimlah. "My son, you are going to be alright! We're going to dress your wound and you will be back to normal in no time." He looked to Zillah, who was now smiling broadly. "Gently, my dear. Wash away the blood so that we can see where he's bleeding from."

She washed and searched, parting his hair and scanning his scalp carefully. She repeated this several times before finally announcing the results with an air of happy bewilderment, "There is not a mark on him!"

Bertlaw was incredulous. "Let me look. With all that blood, there *must* be a cut somewhere." Then, after a search of his own, he sat back on his feet and shook his head before looking back to the servant. "The man said that the *Creator* had healed Rimlah?"

The servant smiled back at him, realizing the old man had spoken the truth. "Yes, Master Bertlaw. That is what he said, among other things. Then he seemingly vanished. I looked for him, but he was gone without a sound."

Bertlaw gave him a quizzical stare before turning back to Rimlah. "Son, it appears you're going to be alright. For now, you should get some rest."

"Father," said Rimlah, now looking a bit more clear-eyed. "We have to go find Tamari. The giant who killed Oresious; I think he took her."

"Did you say 'giant?'" asked Bertlaw with a puzzled expression.

"Yes, Father. There were two of them. I don't know why, but they attacked us before we could escape, "Rimlah drowsily answered.

Bertlaw stood and patted his son on the shoulder reassuringly, "Get some rest for now. We will see what we can do in the morning." With that, he looked back to the servant, "You said, '*among other things*.' Come with me. I need to hear *everything* he said."

After a full briefing, he summoned another servant, "I want you to ride out to Jaylon's house and tell him what has happened. Tell him to meet me at Enoch's house at first light. He will undoubtedly be very worried, but assure him that I will meet him there with the very best of my soldiers. We *will* get Tamari back!" As the servant turned to go out the door, Bertlaw reemphasized, "Make sure he knows that we *will* get her back."

Chapter 15

METHUSELAH WAS LYING IN BED, WIDE AWAKE. HE WASN'T SURE why, but he had been fast asleep one moment and wide awake the next with that same urge to pray for Tamari. He rubbed his eyes and took a deep breath, asking, "Lord, what is happening?"

He sat up and started to slide to his knees beside his bed when he heard the muffled sound of someone talking in the next room. He quietly dressed and opened the door to find his mother on her knees, praying into a chair in the kitchen. He quietly entered the room and placed another chair next to her, sliding down to join her.

His mother looked up at him with tears in her eyes. "You too, Son?"

"Yes, Mother. I get the feeling that Tamari is in some kind of trouble and I should pray for her. What do you think it is?"

She smiled at him reassuringly. "I don't know, but the Lord can see her through it." She wiped away the tears. "With both of us praying, you can be doubly sure of that."

The two of them then began praying out loud, taking turns, imploring the Creator to stand in the gap for this girl they had come to love so much. Sensing the moment, little Mirah slid between them, her little hands clasped like her mother's.

This continued for a while until they heard the sound of a horse and carriage coming into the yard. They rose and went to the door. Methuselah opened it to find a disheveled and, obviously sleep-deprived, Jaylon and Naamah walking gloomily toward the door. Even in the sparse, early-morning light, their sadness was easy to see.

Ednah, immediately empathizing with the apparent pain on Naamah's face, went to her and threw her arms around her in a loving embrace. Naamah, who had so easily evaded a friendship with Ednah for the chance to heighten her own status, quickly let all that fall to the floor and heartily returned the much-needed embrace. They held each other, their shoulders shuddering, for a long moment before Ednah spoke into the back of her new friend's neck, "It will all be alright, whatever it is. The Lord is with us in this. He assures me of that." Ednah gently pushed her back to arm's length with her hands on her heaving shoulders and repeated her assertions, "The Lord has had us up since very early this morning praying for Tamari. We don't know what happened, but we know it will be alright."

Naamah felt a comfort in her heart that she hadn't felt all night, which showed on her face. The truth was that she hadn't felt that type of comfort in a very long time. She had almost forgotten how sweet a spirit this Godly woman had since she had shunned her. Now, looking into those beautiful, gracious eyes, she felt in them a warmth that she vowed to herself never to forsake.

Jaylon watched as the two women instantly kindled their friendship and couldn't help but feel the same kind of sadness for spurning a relationship with these good people. He looked over at the young man he had felt so much disgust for and saw the same kindly expression on his face as his mother. He suddenly felt a pang of regret for the way he had treated him and his family.

Methuselah saw Jaylon looking at him and gently took him by the arm, "Please come in and tell us what has happened."

Jaylon couldn't believe this was the same boy he had helped to humiliate only a few days ago. This same young man, who should hate him, was now treating him with such kindness. "Methuselah, I am sorry for the way I've treated you. I..."

Methuselah cut him off with a wave of his hand, "It is all forgotten. I know you only want the best for Tamari. I think that's why we're all here right now. So, please tell us what has happened."

Jaylon and Naamah settled into the couch and told what they knew as Ednah and Methuselah listened intently.

"That's all we know for now," Jaylon added. "We'll know more when Bertlaw gets here. He said he would be here at first light."

Ednah got up and looked through the window toward the mountain pass through which she knew her husband would be coming, "It's almost light now. I'm sure Bertlaw will be here soon." Then, not knowing how it might sound to them, she added, "Enoch told me that there would be a search party gathering here before he left. He said the Lord told him this. He also said you should not leave on your search until he returns." She turned, saw the puzzled look on her guests' faces, and tried to answer the questions before they came, "You know the Creator speaks to him regularly. He didn't know any more than what I just told you. I only know that we are to wait for him."

Jaylon looked at his wife and put a reassuring hand upon hers, "We know that Enoch is a good man. We will do what he says. His wisdom is something I think we need right now." Naamah nodded her agreement and leaned into his shoulder.

They sat quietly until they heard the sound of many feet marching in unison and coming up the road. Methuselah opened the door to see thirty fully armored soldiers marching three abreast into the yard. The new-day sun was glinting off their bronze breastplates and the tips of their spears high above them. They made their way into the yard and, with the shouting order of what must have been the lead soldier, they lined up in three lines of ten in lock-step fashion.

Methuselah had never seen soldiers marching this way before and was impressed with how they moved in their choreographed strides. Behind them came the equally impressive carriage of Bertlaw with the customary servants in tow. Four of them were ominously carrying a burial box.

Jaylon, Naamah, and Ednah came out of the house and watched as Bertlaw, Zillah, and Rimlah exited the carriage with their customary pomp. Jaylon went over to greet Bertlaw with a scowl on his face, "Bertlaw, I trusted you to get my daughter safely home yesterday! If anything has happened to her..."

Naamah called after him, "Jaylon, don't be rash! Fighting and blaming aren't going to help anythone right now. Let's get her back first. Then we can worry about all that."

Bertlaw took a deep breath and was inwardly glad that Naamah had spoken up. Jaylon was a large man and an imposing figure. He wasn't used to being spoken to that way but decided to swallow his pride and understand his anger, "Jaylon, my friend, I completely understand how you feel. I would feel the same way if I were in your position."

Jaylon gave him a wide-eyed look and growled, "You're *not* in my position! Don't *stand* there and tell me how *you* would feel!"

Bertlaw held up both hands to try and calm the situation, "Jaylon, I didn't mean it that way. I assure you; I couldn't have known anything like this would have happened. I even sent my best swordsman with them to ensure Tamari's safety. The fact is, Oresious gave his *life* to protect her. Even Rimlah was nearly killed trying to protect her."

Methuselah looked at Rimlah and couldn't help but speak up, "He doesn't look to *me* like he was almost killed!" He surprised himself with how much venom seemed to come out with his comment, but it felt good to him, so he kept going, "He doesn't even have a scratch on him! How did you try to protect her, Rimlah? Did you almost die from *running away?*"

Ednah was also surprised at the way Methuselah had reacted. She knew how much he cared for Tamari, but this was more than she could accept. She grabbed him firmly by the arm, turning him to face her, "Methuselah, as Naamah said, fighting and blaming isn't going to help anyone. You weren't there. At least let him explain." Realizing that he had spoken out of his anger toward Rimlah and not his love for Tamari, he relented and calmed himself.

Rimlah walked over and gave him a sorrowful look, "Methuselah, I know you don't like me very much, but I would appreciate it if you would give me a chance to explain what happened."

Methuselah eyed him momentarily, "Alright, go ahead and explain what she was doing with you in the *first* place."

Jaylon spoke up at this point, "Methuselah, don't blame Rimlah for that. Tamari's mother and I wanted her to meet a boy that would be able to give her more than the simple life of a farmer. We wanted her to have a life of privilege and prestige. We only wanted the very best for her. However, you should know, she fought us all the way over it. We *forced* her to go with Rimlah." He walked over and put his hand on Methuselah's shoulder before continuing, "Methuselah, we know how much you care about her and, despite our best efforts; we also know how much she cares about you. I'm sorry for the way we treated you. Please forgive us."

He said it in such a heartfelt way that Methuselah felt sorry for the things he had thought about him. "I think I understand. We all want what's best for Tamari." He looked at Rimlah again, "Alright, Rimlah, please tell us what happened."

Rimlah went through the whole story. He told how he knew Tamari didn't want to go but that she had no choice in the matter. He told how they talked things out and came to an agreement that he was going to treat her better. At this point, he looked Methuselah in the eye, "Methuselah, I promised her that I would talk to you and ask your forgiveness also. I don't have a good excuse for how I've treated you, so I won't attempt to give you one. I only hope you can give me another chance to prove myself."

Methuselah was impressed with how genuine Rimlah seemed but was still a little wary. He looked over to his mother, who nodded her opinion in a way that needed no words. He turned back to Rimlah, took a deep breath, and put his hand on his shoulder, "Rimlah, I've considered you an enemy for a long time, but I believe we could use another friend right now. Please forgive me for what I said earlier."

Rimlah donned a smile that was felt all the way to his soul and agreed.

Jaylon, who had more important things on his mind than how these two boys felt about each other, spoke up, "Alright, now that we've gotten that out of the way, can we please hear the rest of what happened?"

Rimlah began again, "Well, we ate our picnic and were relaxing on the dock when…" He was stopped in his tracks, and his eyes widened as he stared past his listeners into the yard. Everyone turned to see what he was looking at, and an astonished silence came over them.

A huge lion was stepping across the small bridge that spanned the creek. There was something else coming through some of the tall brush beyond, but this lion had everyone's rapt attention. There were lions around the area, but they were usually solitary creatures that rarely ventured onto the farmlands. This particular lion, however, seemed to be walking directly toward them without any sign of guardedness.

The lion got to within about twenty cubits, sat down, and turned toward the commotion in the brush behind him. The onlookers followed suit. There, coming out into the yard, was a behemoth. These were always around too, but it was strange to see one come this close to a homestead, preferring to stay in the swamps instead. However, the most bizarre thing was that this particular behemoth had a very large and frightening-looking giant of a man on its back, riding it like a horse.

They all froze, not knowing what to do or where to go to escape the wrath of such a monstrous man. After a few moments of indecision, the soldiers' captain barked an order, "To arms, to arms! Protect Leader Bertlaw!" Immediately, the soldiers formed a semicircle around the shocked onlookers.

"It's another one!" Rimlah yelled, visibly shaken but too scared to move.

The behemoth, with its rider, climbed out of the creek and stopped next to the lion, who seemed rather bored with the happenings around him. He gave a yawn and lay down, stretching on the cool grass.

The giant looked down at the spectacle before him and gave a hearty and thunderous laugh. "Enoch, I believe we have frightened your friends." He then picked up his fellow rider, who was hidden behind the neck of the behemoth, and spoke to his loyal steed, "Down, Nahla." To everyone's amazement, the hulking creature gently crouched down with its front legs first, then with its hind legs. Then, in one swift movement, the giant swung his leg over the neck of the animal and came to the ground with an earthshaking thud. Then, as gently as a lamb, he put Enoch on his feet before him.

Enoch only smiled at the sight of his guests' gaping mouths, "It is alright, friends. This fellow is not here to harm anyone. He is here to help."

With some difficulty, Enoch was able to explain how he came to know his large friend and who his loyal animal friends were. The problem came in explaining how the Lord spoke to him about the trouble to come and how the Lord had seen fit to cause him and Gardan's paths to cross for just this moment. Jaylon and Naamah were easy to convince, but Bertlaw and Zillah, who had never concerned themselves with the things of the Lord, found the story hard to follow.

"Why should the Creator be so concerned for this girl that he would go through all the trouble to help?" asked Bertlaw. "According to the old stories of Father Adam, the Creator cursed us long ago. Is this not so?"

Enoch thought for a moment about his question before answering, "Bertlaw, when your son does something you told him not to do, you may scold him and punish him for it, but you do not turn your back on him. In fact, nothing he could do would make you stop loving him, would it?"

Bertlaw thought about this, looking over at the son he thought he had lost the night before, then answered, "No, I suppose not."

Enoch nodded. "We are all sons and daughters of the Creator. We were created in the likeness of Him, just as your son has the likeness of you. Even if your son becomes angry and disagrees with you, you will not stop loving him. You may not like what he does, but you will never stop caring for him and wanting what is best for him. In the same way, the Creator punished man's disobedience, but has never, nor will He ever stop caring for us."

Bertlaw and Zillah were impressed with his simple wisdom. They were usually surrounded by people telling them only what they wanted to hear or agreeing sycophantically with whatever they said. But what Enoch said had a ring of truth that challenged their beliefs. It also gave them an almost intangible feeling of warmth within their souls that they were loved in such an unconditional way.

"Enoch, what you say has given me much to think about. I would like to speak to you further on these matters some time," said Bertlaw. "For now, though, I believe we should concentrate on getting Tamari back home." Then, looking at the giant man towering over them, Bertlaw added, "I think your large friend may be interested in what my son has to say about what happened down by the lake."

Rimlah told the story. He had to stop and regain his composure a few times. When he talked about being blindsided by the giant, he stopped and looked at his father, "Should I tell them the rest, Father?"

Bertlaw shook his head, "That may not be important now. We just need to know where to start looking."

"No, Rimlah. Please tell us everything," Enoch said. "Anything you can tell us may help."

Rimlah looked back to his father, who reluctantly agreed. "I woke up to find that I was riding in a cart of some kind. My head hurt so much that I could hardly see, but there was a man in the cart with me who gave me some water and said that I would be alright. I've never seen a man like that before. He was…I'm not sure how else to explain it; beautiful. He was surrounded by light. The light of the sun hurt my eyes, but when I looked at *him*, they didn't hurt. They actually felt better. He told me that the Lord had plans for me and that I should rest. That is all I remember until I woke up again at home when my mother was washing the blood out of my hair."

Bertlaw spoke up again, "My son was badly hurt. He could have been dreaming all of that. As I said, I doubt that any of this is important right now."

Enoch knew that what Rimlah was describing was an angel of the Lord, "Rimlah, you said your mother was washing blood out of your hair. Where were you injured?"

Rimlah shook his head, "That is what I don't understand. I am not injured now in any way. In fact, I woke up this morning feeling better than ever."

Enoch smiled at the boy and raised his hands toward the sky. "Praise be to God!" He then looked back to Rimlah. "That was an angel of the Lord who took care of you in that cart. He told you that the Creator had plans for you and He has healed your wounds. You, Rimlah, are truly blessed!"

Enoch then walked over and put his hand on Bertlaw's shoulder. "My friend, this is exactly what we were discussing earlier. The Lord still truly cares for His children." Bertlaw started to speak but found he had nothing to say. He only gave a slight nod.

After a few moments of quiet, Gardan broke the silence, "We should start our search soon. From what the boy said, it sounds like he ran into my brothers; Syclah and Skaldan. Syclah is not very smart, but he is ruthless. Skaldan is a bit smarter and as evil as anyone has ever been. The girl will not be safe with them for long." He looked at Rimlah and asked, "You say that Syclah was bleeding from his ankle?"

"Yes," replied Rimlah.

Gardan continued, "We should start at the lake then. Syclah will have left us a good trail with which to track him."

They all agreed and prepared to move out. Enoch went over to Bertlaw and Jaylon, "This, I'm afraid, might be a messy business. Your wives should stay here with Ednah until we return." The two men agreed and quietly conferred with the women. Naamah only nodded and walked over and embraced her newfound friend.

Zillah, however, took a bit more convincing, "I do *not* want to stay here with those two farm girls!" This was easily heard by the two "farm girls" in question. "I want to go back *home*! It's not *our* daughter that's missing, and I want Rimlah to come home with me. We almost lost him once over that girl, and I don't want him in any more danger than he has already been subjected to!"

Rimlah, hearing what was being said, marched over and spoke sternly to his mother, "Mother, I *am* going to help find her! You *forced* her to go with me yesterday, and our responsibility was to get her home safely. So, now I'm going to fulfill that responsibility. Besides, I think it might be good for you to spend time with those women. They're good people; perhaps some of their goodness will rub off on *you!*" With that, he turned and joined the others, leaving his mother standing there with her mouth open in shock.

Bertlaw loved his wife, but there were times when she acted in such a manner that he was ashamed of her. This was one of those times. "Zillah, my dear, the wisdom with which your son speaks makes me proud sometimes." He gave her a quick, unwanted kiss on the cheek, turned, and left.

Chapter 16

T AMARI HAD SPENT THE NIGHT ALTERNATING BETWEEN HER feet and her knees. When on her feet, the ropes were just slack enough to lower her arms to a point where they were halfway outstretched, slightly lessening the pain in her burning wrists. However, she was exhausted from the previous day's ordeal and, when she couldn't stand any longer, elected the only other option; her knees. In this position, her arms were stretched straight out. The pressure on her wrists was excruciating, not to mention the pain in her knees, which were being cut into upon the rocky ground between the two unyielding trees.

She had managed to drift off a few times during the night, though she couldn't be sure if it was sleep or if she had only passed out from the searing pain. She had cried for the better part of the evening but, noting the apparent pleasure her fears seemed to elicit from her monstrous captors, finally decided not to give in to them any longer. Besides, she was growing tired of the sound of her own sobs.

Her gruesome abductors had spent the evening laughing and discussing their plans for the "puny little men" who they thought would surely be coming to rescue her. They sharpened their swords and took turns capturing unsuspecting forest animals, cutting them in two, and throwing the remains at her feet. She would kick them away in horror and plead for them to stop.

This, however, only brought forth more cackles of delight from these twisted goons.

She felt so alone and wondered if anyone would find her at all. "If they did, would they even be able to rescue me?" she thought. "How would anyone even be able to defeat such monsters?" It seemed to her that all hope was gone.

Then, a quiet voice from out of nowhere whispered in her ear, "Pray, Child." She stopped and looked around to see where it came from. She saw nothing. The almost inaudible voice spoke again, softly and gently, "Pray, Child. Pray as you've seen Methuselah and his family pray. I am the Creator of all things, and I love you. Do not give up hope, for nothing is impossible to Me."

She was suddenly awash with new hope. An indescribable feeling of warmth fell over her, especially given the circumstances. She had no better ideas, so she began to pray. She continued to do so throughout her fitful night. This would have to give her the strength to get through this ordeal. This would have to be her new source of strength from this point forward. She knew only that she didn't have it within herself anymore.

The search party arrived at the lake's edge and followed the path along the banks toward the dock where Rimlah said they were attacked. As they drew nearer, Rimlah became increasingly fidgety and nervous. Methuselah couldn't help but notice. About one hundred cubits away, Rimlah stopped and stared out over the lake, not wanting to look toward the place where what was left of the carriage, horses, and Oresious lay. Methuselah put an understanding hand on his shoulder. "Rimlah, it's alright if you want to stay back here. We know this will be difficult for you."

"I'm alright," he said with a quivering voice. "I just… It's just that…" He took another deep breath and started again, "Oresious was like a father to me when my own father was too busy to act like one. I know that sounds horrible, but sometimes I felt like I was a disappointment to my father. Oresious never made me feel that way. He always seemed to understand me. I loved him, and he died trying to protect me. My father spends most of his time protecting his reputation." He paused and wiped away the tears that were forming in his eyes. "It's not going to be easy for me to say goodbye to Oresious, that's all."

Methuselah put his arm around his shoulder. "I understand. Take your time. I'll give you a few moments to yourself." With that, Methuselah walked to where the rest of the group was surveying the gruesome scene.

It was all laid out before them like the aftermath of a giant child's tantrum. For the longest time, no one said a word. They just stood and wondered at the carnage. Even the soldiers, who had yet to be tested by battle, were visibly shaken by what they saw.

Bertlaw got down from his carriage and walked over to where his most trusted servant lay, dissected and mangled. He stared momentarily before his knees buckled, and he fell to the ground.

The captain, who himself was a bit sickened by the sight, was the first to speak as he came to his master's aide, "Master Bertlaw, please let me help you back to your carriage. My men will take good care of our dear friend, Oresious." He helped Bertlaw to his feet and walked him back toward the carriage, where the other servants helped him get reseated. Then, the captain motioned for his men to get the burial box that Bertlaw's servants had been carrying.

Rimlah finally made his way to the scene. Seeing what was left of Oresious, he immediately turned and ran to the lake's edge and vomited. He stayed there for a while, allowing time for the soldiers to do their work. Slowly, he came to his feet and joined his father in the carriage.

His father spoke softly, "Rimlah, my son, I know what Oresious meant to you. He meant a great deal to me as well. He was a good man." Bertlaw gently turned his son's face toward his own and continued with a sincerity that Rimlah had never seen in his father's face, "He was actually a better man than I in many ways. We will all miss him very much." Rimlah put his arms around his father and sobbed deeply into his chest. It was the closest he had ever felt to him, and it felt good under the circumstances.

The rest of the men continued to survey the area and gave the father and son their privacy. Jaylon was looking at the horses, shaking his head. "How powerful must these giants be to cut through them like that?"

Gardan, who was studying the tracks they left, answered, "They are not only powerful but ruthless."

Enoch nodded to his giant friend before calling to the captain, who had gone back to studying the scene himself, "Captain, what are your thoughts?"

The captain had picked up Oresious' sword and was examining it closely. "I can see that Rimlah was correct. There is blood on the tip of his sword, and you can see where one of them had fallen and bled there for a while before getting back up and dragging himself up the road that way." he said, pointing with the sword toward the road that led away from the lake. "There should be an easy trail to follow."

Rimlah was now climbing down and out of the carriage, having regained his composure. "Yes. That was the direction we ran to get away. Let's move on and I will show you where we were when they found us." With that, Rimlah started leading the way.

After the men had left, the women went inside the house. The mood was tense, given Zillah's childish performance outside. However, like many of the more well-to-do women of her station, she quickly forgave herself and simply assumed that the two "farm girls'" feelings didn't really matter anyway.

Zillah had walked around the house and scanned the sparse, utilitarian décor with an unmistakable air of disdain. She would pick up one of the few little knick-knacks and mementos displayed here and there, remarking with a little, "Hm." Then, she would put it back down and flutter her fingers into the air as if to brush off the nonexistent filth she assumed she had just soiled herself with.

Ednah was quite aware of what Zillah was implying but graciously chose not to be offended. Naamah was also aware, but she found herself embarrassed for Ednah's sake, whispering to her, "I'm sorry." Ednah just shook her head with an understanding smile and went into the kitchen to prepare a snack of fruits for her guests.

Bored with her surroundings, Zillah decided to sprawl out on the only couch in the humble home and close her eyes as if to shut out the ugliness around her. This forced Ednah and Naamah to stay in the kitchen where the only other chairs were. Ednah had finished cutting the fruit and arranged them neatly on a simple plate the three women could share.

Ednah looked over at the lounging Zillah and then back to her even more embarrassed friend, Naamah. In her sweetest voice, she invited Zillah to join them, "Zillah, I've made a fruit plate for us if you would like some." Without a word or opening her eyes, Zillah threw her hand over the back of the couch, palm up, as if to say, "Just bring it to me."

Naamah looked at Ednah with shock. Ednah, however, didn't skip a beat and spoke with all the tact of a royal dignitary, "Zillah, dear, won't you please join us at the table. I wouldn't want you to accidentally stain that beautiful dress you're wearing. We have another chair here for you."

Zillah didn't speak. She only took an exaggerated deep breath and got up, demonstrating openly that it was a bother to her. She walked over to the table and, instead of sitting next to Naamah where the other chair was, pulled it over to the head of the table, thus, continuing to show herself above the stature of these two peasants with which she was forced to spend time.

For a little while, over their snack, Ednah and Naamah tried to make small talk with Zillah to make her feel more comfortable with them. Still, they could only elicit a few one-word answers here and there from her. Meanwhile, Zillah picked through the plate of fruit, shoving the pieces she didn't want out of her way and eating only the choicest pieces herself. When she had gotten her fill, she rose and resumed her position on the couch without a word, much less a "Thank you."

Ednah thought to herself, "This is going to be a long day. Lord, please give me patience."

Chapter 17

AFTER SURVEYING WHERE THE OLD MAN IN THE GARDENER'S cart had found Rimlah, the search party followed the blood trail and drag marks left by Syclah. The group was rather somber, each man mulling over what would come. They were still determining precisely what they would be coming against when they reached their destination. The soldiers were nervous and a bit anxious due to what they had seen by the lake. Bertlaw, looking over his fine fighting force, had an air of confidence. Jaylon was understandably worried about his daughter's safety, and, for that matter, so were Methuselah and Rimlah. And Gardan was quietly reflecting on what he would do when he confronted his monstrously evil kinsmen again after all the years of peaceful seclusion he had found with his animal friends.

Enoch was somber also, but not in a nervous way. He kept quiet and off to himself, spending most of his time in deep thought and prayer. He pled for Tamari's safety and the protection of all the men in the party.

It was a little after midday when they finally reached a point where the trail led to the base of a low mountain and continued toward the peak. Enoch raised a hand in the air, and the group stopped behind a stand of large trees that would conceal them from anyone who might be watching for their arrival. Gardan dismounted Nahla and came to where Enoch was standing.

Gardan quietly said, "Enoch, my friend, I believe we have found what we seek. They have taken the high ground. They are undoubtedly setting a trap for us up there. They will have a definite advantage against us if we go to them."

Enoch noticed the uneasiness in his giant friend's voice. It seemed strange for a man as large and powerful as this. Still, it was perfectly understandable, knowing what had happened the last time Gardan had seen his brothers. He turned toward the group and spoke, "We need to stop and think about this for a moment. My friend, Gardan, has pointed out the fact that our prey is waiting for us to come to them. He believes we would be walking into an obvious trap if we rushed headlong up the mountain. We need to carefully consider our next move."

The captain spoke up, "I agree. If they are up there, they will have the tactical advantage of fighting on their own terms. In my opinion, it would be a mistake to do so."

"But my *daughter* is up there with those vile beasts!" Jaylon yelled with disgust. "We cannot wait for them to come to us. Who knows what they may do to her if we leave her up there any longer." Until now, he had held his emotions in check but couldn't hold them back anymore. With tears flowing, he dropped to his knees and cried into his hands, "They may have killed her already."

Enoch walked over to him and put a caring hand on his shoulder. "Jaylon, my friend, the Lord would not have had us go through all of this just to bring your daughter back dead. I believe He will show Himself strong and faithful in our weakness. Do not lose faith now."

Jaylon looked up at him through his tears, "Enoch, my friend, I'm afraid I traded my faith for prestige and notoriety a long time ago. I do not think the Creator will listen to me anymore."

Enoch smiled down at him and shook his head. "Jaylon, all He wants is our love. Just as you love your daughter and want nothing more than to have her back, the Lord feels the same way about you. No matter how far away you think you are, it only takes one step of faith to come back to Him. Pray to him to take you back and to bring your daughter back to you. You might be surprised at what He will do."

Enoch then turned back to the rest of the search party. "Give me a while to speak with the Lord about our situation. Stay here. I'll be back." With that, he turned and walked into the trees. The soldiers gave each other quizzical looks as they watched him go, Leeno following close behind.

Enoch had walked several hundred Cubits into the forest until he found a nice secluded spot to stop and pray. He got on his knees and began to implore the Lord for an answer. He had prayed only a few moments before he heard a soothing voice speaking to him, "Enoch, I hear your prayers and am pleased with your faithfulness."

Enoch opened his eyes and was surprised to see Leeno sitting directly before him. He looked around to see if the Lord was elsewhere but could find no one else. Then, he was taken aback to realize that it was Leeno, Himself, who was speaking, "Enoch, do not be alarmed. I can take any form I choose to speak with you. In fact, I have taken this very form to show Gardan My love for many years now. He does not realize this yet, but he is not ready to fully embrace Me as he still carries the scars of his father, Azazel. His father taught him nothing but hate and evil, but he is a special creation all his own that is capable of so much more."

"Yes, Father. He is a good man, and has been a good friend to me. However, he is becoming aware of You and has asked me questions as to who and what You are. He told me that You appeared to him in a dream. I believe that made a great impression on him."

The Great Lion gave a slight chuckle, "Yes. I wanted to see if he would respond to Me. I am happy to see that he did. He will, one day, be a man of great faith."

Enoch smiled widely. "Thank you, Lord. I am grateful that You have chosen to take such an interest in him." Enoch's countenance became more serious as he continued, "Lord, I ask You to please help my friend, Jaylon. He feels as if You have turned Your back on him because of his lack of faith. He feels like You won't love him because he has chosen to ignore You for the last few years. I know he has lost his way, but I ask You to please help him find it again."

"He is, at this very moment, in prayer to Me. I have already forgiven him. As for the rest of the men with you, I am about to show them My power by delivering Tamari back to safety. This is what I want you to do."

⌁

When Enoch returned and told them the plan, everyone thought he was insane. Before leaving, he went over to Jaylon. He smiled widely, saying, "Jaylon, the Lord told me He has already forgiven you. You need only trust Him now. Have faith, for you will have your daughter back safely today."

With that, he turned and walked up the mountain path- alone.

Chapter 18

THE SWIFT-FOOTED, BEODAN WAS CHARGED WITH THE JOB OF the lookout. Azazel had given him this duty because he would have the ability to watch for any would-be rescuers from halfway down the mountain and, within seconds, run back up and alert them of the coming hoards that their foes would most likely assemble against them.

He had been there for a long time and was growing quite bored when something caught his eye. He could just make out the figure of a man coming up the path at the base of the mountain. He waited to see how many were with him. He kept waiting. Finally, satisfied that he was alone, Beodan gleefully giggled, "This foolish little man comes alone? What does he think he can do alone? Hee-hee. Wait 'till I tell Father!" He then turned and bounded up the mountain with blinding speed.

Enoch climbed about a third of the way up the mountain path when he encountered the two helpers the Creator had promised him. They were huge men with glowing, golden and blemish-less skin. He had seen the Lord's angels before but was always awed by their appearance. One had shoulder-length blonde hair, and the other had darker hair that flowed halfway down his back.

They stood a cubit taller than Enoch and were flawlessly built and muscular with large, perfectly white wings folded behind their backs. At their sides hung glimmering, golden-handled swords enclosed in what seemed to be solid pearl sheathes bejeweled with at least twelve types of stones, some of which Enoch had never seen before. They were altogether both beautiful and fierce in appearance.

As Enoch approached them, they smiled down at him through dazzling teeth. "Enoch, most favored of men, the Creator sent us to aid you in collecting the girl. Follow us and be sure to stay behind us at all times. Do this and you will be safe."

Enoch responded happily, "I will do exactly as you say, my beautiful friends. I am thankful the Lord has sent you to help me retrieve this poor girl. She must be terribly frightened."

"She is," The dark-haired angel responded. "However, she is not alone. The Lord has been with her from the start. He has kept her from any undue harm."

Enoch smiled, "Then, let's go get her." He followed close behind them, praying his thanks to God the whole way.

When Beodan came rushing into camp, his father and brothers were excited by the prospect of what they thought was the news of the coming battle. When he told them that only one man was coming, the excitement in Azazel's eyes turned quickly to anger and disappointment. "They dare to send one man up!? Do they think they can talk their way into rescuing this girl?"

Then Azazel calmed and asked, "What did the man look like?"

Beodan shook his head and answered dumbly, "He was a long way down the mountain, Father. I didn't see him good enough to know what he looked like."

Azazel glared at him momentarily, then stroked his wispy black beard. "If only one man is coming up here, he is either a fool or very wise. Perhaps the lone man is our true prey, Enoch." Then, with new excitement, he started barking out a new game plan to his henchmen.

Tamari watched all the happenings with great interest and fear for the brave soul walking up the mountain to what must be certain death. She prayed quietly, "Lord, please protect him."

Enoch entered the encampment behind his angelic escorts. As they came into the open, the angels pulled their silver-bladed swords, which now appeared to be ablaze with an ethereal blue flame, and opened their wings wide to shield Enoch from sight. If Enoch could have seen beyond them, he would have seen five of the largest, ugliest, and most frightening men he had ever witnessed, all standing with drawn swords. In front of them, he would have seen a small, bearded, ominous-looking man with an astonished, disbelieving look standing with his mouth opened and eyes wide.

Enoch looked to his right and saw Tamari tied up between the two trees and on her knees with her arms outstretched. She looked at him and then to where her giant captors were, then back at him, then back to them, as if she didn't understand something. She gave him a look that seemed to him both elation and terror.

Azazel, who had, up to now, been dumbstruck, was finally able to speak, "What do *you two* want? I have no business with *you!*" Skaldan and his brothers just gave him a befuddled look for a moment, then exchanged unknowing glances with each other as their father continued to talk to what seemed to be an empty space, "You two are *not* welcome here! Your Master threw my brothers and me down to this miserable place, and we have made it our own! Do you hear me?"

The two angelic warriors remained silent. Enoch had stopped where he stood when Azazel began to speak, but the angel to his right motioned with one of his hands to tell him not to stop. As he moved closer to Tamari, the angel sidestepped along to continue giving him the wing cover.

Skaldan was confused by his father's odd behavior. "Father, who are you talking to? There is no one here," he continued, scanning the encampment in case he was missing something.

Azazel angrily hissed at him, "Quiet, Boy!" Then, he continued ranting at his unseen and uninvited guests, "Do you have a message for me or does your Master want to apologize for His treatment of me and my brothers? Oh," he said with a little snicker. "I know what He has sent you here for. He wants to beg me not to harm His precious little servant boy, Enoch."

He waited for their reply but resumed his haranguing, venomous insults when it didn't come, "Perhaps the Creator wants to strike a deal with me for his life. Is that it? Well, He can *forget it!* As soon as that little man gets here, he is as good as dead!" Still, no reaction.

This non-responsiveness was making him angrier with every moment. He drew his sword, which looked flimsy in comparison to those of the angelic warriors, and started to take a step forward but found that his feet wouldn't move. He got even angrier, "What do you think you're doing!?" He tried again to no avail. Then, he started jerking at his feet with all his strength to free them from this invisible hold.

His sons eyed him as if he had gone mad, doing this odd little dance before them. Syclah, who wasn't bright enough to know not to, began chuckling and pointing at him, "Dat's funny, Fadder! Hee-hee. You look funny!" Azazel twisted around and shot him a look that made him stop immediately.

Skaldan, tempted to laugh at this strange sight, asked his father, "What are you doing, and who are you talking to?"

Azazel was livid by now, "I am talking to those two angels of the Creator, and they have made it so I cannot move my feet! Help me you fool!"

Skaldan started toward his father. His upper body momentum had started forward before he realized that his feet were also stuck to the ground. He fell right on top of Azazel with a bone-crushing thud, pinning him underneath. Syclah then laughed again and wanted to go over and see the spectacle close-up. He then followed suit by falling on his face. This caused him to stretch out his previously-cut ankle. The pain of this stopped all his laughter immediately. The other three brothers had seen enough and tried to pick up their feet. They couldn't.

Although Enoch couldn't see what was happening, he could hear it all. After finally untying the bewildered Tamari, he tried to steal a glance at what was happening. All he could see under the angel's wing was a red-faced little man underneath a giant resembling Gardan.

He whispered to Tamari, "Can you walk, Child?"

Tamari looked at him like he was water in a desert and replied, "If it's away from *here*, I can!"

He helped her up, and they quickly made an exit. They made their way down the rocky trail for a while without saying a word. Enoch slowed his pace so Tamari wouldn't hurt herself trying to keep up with him. Finally, Enoch broke the silence, "Tamari, I am very proud of you for being strong in that horrifying situation. I know you must have been terrified."

She didn't speak for a few moments. Then, she slowed her pace and eventually stopped. Enoch turned to see the tears welling up in her eyes. He put his arms gently around her and spoke softly, "You don't have to be strong now, Dear. Go ahead and let it out."

She hugged him tightly and wailed into his chest, letting out all the anguished emotions she desperately tried to hide from her unfeeling captors. Enoch just held her and wept for this girl he had come to love like a daughter.

After a short time, Enoch became aware of a presence and looked up to see one of the angels standing in the path, watching them. He thought that they would have to hurry and cut short this emotional time out, but the angel had a look of compassion in his eyes that told Enoch that it was alright. After her crying had eased, Enoch pulled back and wiped her tears from her eyes. "Are you ready to move on now, Child?" She nodded, and they turned toward the angel, who appeared to have been enjoying the moment of compassionate love he had just witnessed.

"Enoch, you and Tamari can take your time getting down the mountain. The other warrior is standing watch over Azazel and his evil offspring. They will be stuck there until tomorrow." Then, to Enoch's surprise, he turned and addressed Tamari directly, "Tamari, your prayers were heard. The Creator sent us because of your faithfulness in the face of great danger."

Enoch looked at Tamari and saw an expression of shock as the angel continued, "The Lord, your God, says to tell you that He has great plans for you. He will bless you and your offspring will outnumber the stars in the heavens. After the Earth is cleansed of its evil, it will be your grandchildren who will repopulate the world. You shall be very blessed indeed."

Tamari was still somewhat shocked as she heard the message and couldn't form the words for a response. The angel only gave her an understanding smile and turned back to Enoch. "Enoch, the Creator says that you should take the search party back and gather their families in Urna. The Lord is going to use this opportunity to do a mighty work for all the people there to see that they might know that He loves them."

Enoch agreed. "Thank you, my friend. We will do as the Lord has said." With that, they continued down the mountain.

Chapter 19

ZILLAH HAD FALLEN ASLEEP ON THE COUCH AND REMAINED there most of the day. Naamah and Ednah had used the quiet time to build upon their new friendship until Mirah woke up. Ednah quietly fed her, and the two women took her outside, allowing Zillah to sleep.

Naamah had never spent time with Mirah, and it was a nice distraction for her to get her mind off her worries. She spent a while playing pretend with her and listening to her songs. The songs only made sense to Mirah, but Naamah truly enjoyed hearing them and watching her walk around, raising her hands high in the air for emphasis during certain parts of the songs.

However, eventually, it only served to remind her of Tamari when she was little and sang her own songs. That was when the tears returned, and Ednah had to console her again. With her sweet spirit, Mirah also tried to comfort her with an innocent pat on her hand, "Are you alwite?"

Naamah couldn't help a little laugh and answered her, "Yes, Dear. I just miss my own little girl. She is a sweetheart, just like you." Mirah smiled at her and went back to her song.

Ednah could see that Naamah was very tired. "Naamah, would you like to lie down for a while? You can use Mirah's bedroom. You can shut the door and it'll be nice and quiet for you. I know you didn't sleep much last night."

Naamah nodded and smiled a pained smile at her, "Yes. Thank you."

—⁓—

The sun was just descending below the horizon when Enoch and Tamari reached the base of the mountain. The group stared in amazement at the sight of them unharmed.

When Tamari saw the group, she smiled until she noticed the hulking giant behind them and standing beside a behemoth. She stopped in her tracks and screamed, "Look out behind you! It's another one!" She then jumped behind Enoch, who was surprised by her reaction until he realized he had neglected to tell her about Gardan.

He put his arm around her and said gently, "Tamari, I am sorry. I forgot to tell you about Gardan. He is an old friend who has come to help us. I assure you that he can be trusted. In fact, I trust him with my life."

She slowly came from behind Enoch and eyed the giant man warily. "Are you sure? He looks like them."

Enoch reassured her, "Yes. He is their brother, but I promise you that he dislikes them just as much as you do."

Gardan tried to give her the friendliest smile before speaking, "I can tell you; I probably dislike them *even more* than you do." Then he turned and introduced his even larger friend, "This is Nahla. She and I are both at your service." Then Nahla, as if on cue, gently brought her massive head down to Tamari and let her pet her on the face. As she rubbed her, the behemoth gave a loud purr that sounded like that of a massive kitten, causing Tamari to giggle at her.

Gardan introduced his other friend, saying, "And this furry fellow is Leeno." Leeno slowly came over, gently rubbed along her side, and licked her rope-chaffed wrist while letting out a purr of his own. Tamari cautiously scratched behind his ear and giggled again.

Unable to keep his composure, Jaylon threw all dignity to the wind as he ran to his daughter and embraced her, almost knocking her down. Neither father nor daughter spoke as they held each other, sobbing. Words were not needed at the moment.

Tears fell from many of the eyes watching this reunion—even some of the soldiers. Methuselah approached his father and put his arm around him, fighting his own happy tears for their safe return. "Father, I am glad to see you safely back. I see that the Lord protected you well."

"Yes," Enoch answered with a laugh. "I want to tell you all what a great thing the Creator has just done and also what He says He will do in the near future." He said this so that everyone could hear. They all perked up their ears and gathered around to hear Enoch's story. He looked over to Tamari, who was now wiping away some of her tears and approaching where Methuselah and Rimlah stood. Methuselah met her halfway and hugged her gently, whispering his love into her ear.

A few days before, Jaylon wanted her to have nothing to do with this "simple farm boy." He only wanted this precious daughter he almost lost to be happy, and she was obviously happy with Methuselah. Now he just watched with an appreciative and agreeable smile on his face. He now saw that Methuselah cared deeply for her, and she for him. He vowed to himself never to stand in the way of their love again.

After they loosened their embrace, Tamari saw Rimlah looking at her with moist eyes and a pained expression. He met her gaze and then looked down, feeling ashamed. "I am so very sorry, Tamari. I'm sorry I got you into this whole mess."

She touched his face, bringing it up to look into his eyes. "Do not blame yourself, Rimlah. How could you have known what would happen? *No one* could have known. Besides, we're friends now, and although I would have rather it had happened in a much less adventurous way, I'm glad it did." Rimlah finally nodded and gave her an approving smile.

The captain was watching all this appreciatively but couldn't keep his curiosity at bay any longer, "I do not mean to be insensitive, but Enoch, what happened up there?"

Enoch laughed and then looked back to Tamari. "I believe our newly-freed Tamari should tell us what happened to her first. I will pick it up where I came into the story."

Tamari eyed them all, took a deep breath, and told everything that she had gone through without leaving out anything. When she told them how many giants were at the top of the mountain, the group's mood returned to somberness. This was especially true of Gardan, who only listened quietly and thoughtfully stared up toward the mountain.

When she came to the part story where Enoch came in, they both took turns with the telling. She finally told them about the angel who met them on the path down the mountain. At this point, Enoch gently touched her shoulder, "Perhaps, some things are better to keep to yourself for now." She thought about that for a moment and nodded her agreement.

Enoch then gave them the last message the angel had relayed to him. "The angel said that we should all gather together in Urna. He said that the Lord was going to show His love for all the people of Urna. I do not know in what way He is going to do this but, it will, no doubt, involve Gardan's brothers up there. When the angel releases them tomorrow, they will surely be very angry and looking for revenge. So, let us go and gather our families tonight and meet back up in the city."

Bertlaw now spoke up, "The soldiers already have places to stay in Urna. However, Enoch, You, Jaylon, and Gardan do not. I would be honored if you would stay in my house tonight." Then he thought about what he had just said. "Gardan, you may not be able to stay in my house, but you are definitely welcome to stay at my house." This elicited a chuckle from everyone.

Before leaving, Gardan spoke to Tamari, "Tamari, I've been riding Nahla most of the day and could use a good walk. How would you like to ride her back? I think she would really like it if you would."

She looked at her father, who nodded his approval, then back to Gardan, "I would *love* to, but only if Methuselah can ride with me."

Gardan gave a hearty laugh, "Of course, he can." With that, he commanded, "Nahla, down!" The colossal beast brought her head low to allow them to climb up. They made their way to her back, with the caring hands of Gardan helping and guiding them the whole way.

The group then started heading back to Enoch's house. The mood, for some, was a little lighter now that Tamari was safe. Jaylon, of course, was happy to have his daughter back. Rimlah's conscience was now relieved. Bertlaw felt like he had done his civic duty by marshaling his soldiers to fight against the evil at hand. He looked forward to marching them back into the city as their triumphant General. The fact that they hadn't done any fighting was unfortunate. Still, for a skilled orator like himself, he would easily accentuate his leadership during the retelling.

However, Enoch was still in a somewhat somber mood. He was happy that Tamari was safe but also a bit anxious about what the next day would bring. Gardan was quiet and uneasy about seeing his brothers again.

The most solemn of the group was the captain. He silently hoped that this Creator Enoch spoke of was indeed as powerful as he said. Instead of going to fight two giants in open combat, he was now looking at the prospect of protecting the entire city from five of these ruthless foes with a group of inexperienced soldiers, who he wasn't so sure were ready for battle. Looking at them, he could see the same fear and worry in their eyes. They would need all the help they could get.

Chapter 20

METHUSELAH WAS ELATED. HE HAD ALWAYS DREAMED OF being able to tame one of the enormous beasts that roamed the earth. His attempt at riding the leviathan had failed miserably. He had decided then to not try that again, heeding his father's advice. Now he was actually riding a behemoth! He had never imagined that the ride would be so smooth.

He was amazed at how gentle Nahla was. It was as if she really enjoyed having her tiny passengers aboard, every so often trumpeting her pride with guttural wails so loud they scared Tamari, causing her to squeal with delight and laughter.

Methuselah thought he had regained the world, having his Love back with him and hearing her wonderful voice again. "Tamari, I am so happy you're back safe again. I was so worried about you. I love you very much."

Tamari melted back into his strong arms with a contented sigh. "I love you too, Methuselah." She thought for a moment and turned to look back at him. "I'm sorry about what happened at my house before. I was worried when that giant took me up there that I would never see you again. I was worried that I wouldn't get the chance to explain what happened." She took a deep breath before continuing, "I know you must have been very upset, seeing me standing with Rimlah and having everyone laughing at you like that."

Methuselah had almost forgotten the whole episode until she brought it up again. "I was upset for a while." Truth be told, he was still a little angry about it now that he had relived the moment in his mind. "Your father asked me for help with the fish grinder, and Dolan poured the ground fish all over me! Why did he do that? All I was doing was trying to help." He now became more animated, speaking with his hands, "Then, Dolan led me to that bird bath to wash the fish from my eyes. The next thing I knew, I was standing there with fish guts all over me, and all those people were laughing at me! Worst of all, I saw you standing there, all dressed up, and next to Rimlah, who I didn't really care for at the time." He huffed and shook his head. "What was going on, Tamari? Why did they do that to me?"

Tamari explained as best she could, "My parents wanted me to spend time with Rimlah because his father is rich and influential in Urna. Since they found emeralds on our property, they have changed a lot. They know that I love you, Methuselah, but they said they wanted more for me than what they think you can provide, so they thought that if they could embarrass you, I would be embarrassed of you too. It didn't work, though. I was so angry at them for what they did to you." She was getting upset herself at this point. She took a deep breath to calm down before continuing, "Then, the next day, I wanted to come to you and apologize, but they made me go with them to Bertlaw's house. They didn't even tell me where we were going until we arrived." Now she was speaking with her hands.

"Then, as if it weren't bad enough, they arranged for me and Rimlah to go on a picnic down by the lake. We were able to talk things out and I told him that I love you. I told him that there was no chance of him and me ever having anything else. He apologized and understood that. After talking to him after a while, I actually realized that he isn't so bad after all. There is another side to him that you don't see when he is around those idiot friends of his. Anyway, he promised me that he wouldn't act like that anymore and said he would apologize to you for the way he treated you."

Then, she thought about what had happened next. The thought was like a punch in the face, and she started to cry, "Poor Oresious. He was so brave." She cried into her hands while Methuselah gently comforted her.

After a while, Methuselah thought he heard her giggling. "What is it?" he asked her, a bit confused.

She picked her head up and wiped away her tears. "You looked pretty funny with all that fish juice in your face."

He giggled a little himself, just glad that she was smiling again. "Let me pour fish juice in your face and you would look pretty funny yourself."

They went back to enjoying the ride again. Methuselah looked over at Gardan, who was quietly walking beside them, "Gardan, could I ask you a question?"

Gardan was jolted from his deep thoughts, "What?"

Methuselah asked again, "Could I ask you something?"

Gardan smiled broadly at him, "Son of Enoch, you may ask me anything you wish."

Methuselah smiled back at him, impressed at how friendly this giant man was. "How is it that you have befriended your two animal companions? Behemoths and lions usually tend to shy away from people, but these two seem to truly love you."

Gardan thought carefully about his question before answering, "Methuselah, I suppose I have always had a way with animals of all kinds, but I think the real reason is that I loved them first. I treat them as I would want to be treated." He rubbed Nahla on her neck and continued, "Nahla here was stuck in the mud up to her belly when I found her. She hadn't eaten for many days and was very weak. I brought her food and eventually was able to get her out. She was very appreciative, and has never left my side since. She is free to go any time she wants to. I would never make her stay with me, but she chooses to stay. I am very lucky to have her. She has been a good friend to me."

He then reached down and rubbed the back of Leeno's neck. "This little fellow has been with me for a long time. He just showed up one day when I was feeling very lonely. I don't know why he chose me, but I feel very fortunate to have him also. He came to me when I had no one else. He has been closer than a brother to me. I believe he would give his life for me, and I would not hesitate to do the same for him."

Methuselah was impressed. "You really do have a way with them. I can see that you care deeply for them." He then got a sheepish grin on his face, "I'm not as good with animals as you are. I tried to befriend a leviathan, but it didn't go very well."

Gardan let out a howling belly laugh. "Yes, your father told me about that." He laughed again, "He said he took you for quite a ride."

Tamari laughed a little now, and Methuselah's face turned red, "Well… I thought that if I could just…"

Gardan put up his hand to stop him from trying to give an explanation where he knew there wouldn't be a good one, "Methuselah, my young friend, you must show them love before they will trust you and show you love. You cannot force an animal to do your will. You must show them you care first. Then, they may decide to do what you want."

Methuselah was a bit confused, "But we have oxen that do our will on the farm. We make them do what we want them to do."

"Some animals are easier to tame than others," answered Gardan. "But, do you not feed and water them first? You showed them that you cared before they did your will."

Methuselah thought about that for a moment and nodded, "You are very wise, Gardan. I can see why my father likes you."

Gardan smiled at him and chuckled, "Thank you, son of Enoch. Your father is wiser than I. If you listen to him, you will gain that wisdom for yourself."

Darkness had enveloped the little house, and Ednah was busily preparing a meal for her guests in the kitchen. Mirah was doing her best to be a good little helper but spent much of her time dancing about, singing to her funny songs.

Zillah had spent the better part of her day sleeping but now opened her eyes to see two big blue eyes staring back at her. When Zillah's eyes opened, Mirah let out a playful squeal and ran back into the kitchen, laughing and hiding behind her mother's legs. Seemingly out of character, Zillah had to laugh at the cuteness of it. She hadn't had a little one around in a long time and had to admit to herself that she missed the joy she felt when Rimlah had played the same sort of games when he was a child.

She slowly stretched and sat up on the couch, looking into the kitchen to see what Ednah was doing. As she watched her move about and set plates on the table, Zillah was impressed at how Ednah carried herself. She had spent a lot of time around the wealthier women of Urna who possessed all the social graces that women of that status needed to get invited to the finest parties and city events. However, Ednah had a quality that none of those women had. She had an inner peace—a quiet dignity—an innate beauty that almost made her glow.

As she pondered these things, she was suddenly aware that she was being watched from behind by those big blue eyes again. Zillah quickly turned her head to see her, causing Mirah to squeal and run back to the safety of her mother's legs again.

Ednah patted her on the head and laughed, "Are you bothering Zillah again?"

"No," came the sheepish reply. "I'm playing wif her."

"Well, maybe Zillah doesn't want to play with you," she said as she continued setting the table.

Zillah stood and staggered into the kitchen while she stretched again. "It's alright. I needed to get up anyway. I suppose I have not been a very polite guest, sleeping all day like I have."

Ednah was slightly surprised at how civil Zillah was speaking to her now compared to how she had begun the day. "I understand. I'm sure you had a long night with all the trauma of Rimlah coming home the way he did. I would have been just as tired after a night like that."

Zillah thoughtfully watched Mirah as she resumed her little song and dance routine, "She is an adorable child." She hesitated a moment before finishing her thought, "It has been a long time since I have been around a small child like this. If it weren't so much work, I would have to say that I miss it in a way."

Ednah smiled and looked at Mirah. "Yes. She can be a handful, but she and her brother have been a blessing to us. The Lord has been very good to us to trust us to raise them."

Zillah gave her a strange look before asking, "How do you mean that the Lord has 'trusted' you to raise them? Are they not *your* children?"

Ednah hadn't even thought about how she had phrased the statement until now and had to think for a moment before answering, "Well, Enoch and I see our children as gifts from the Lord. We have been entrusted with raising them, but they, like all people, actually belong to the Lord to begin with. We are merely caretakers, charged with the duty to bring them up in the knowledge of the Creator."

Zillah had never heard such things before and seemed confused by them. "You have a strange way of seeing things."

Ednah smiled at her and offered her a chair at the table. "I understand how it may sound strange to you, but it actually makes perfect sense." She thought for a moment before continuing, "Zillah, your father gave you to be married to Bertlaw—to be his wife—but that doesn't change the fact that you are still your father's daughter. Your father entrusted Bertlaw to care for you and provide for your needs, but if you went to your father and asked something of him, would he not help you?"

Zillah thought about that. "That is true, but it's not the same thing. My father is there for me to go to. The 'Creator', as you call Him, is not around for us to go to. What has He to do with us? If He cares for us at all, He has chosen not to show it."

Ednah sensed the pain in Zillah's voice. "You may think that the Lord doesn't care about you or your needs, but did He not bring your son back to you last night unharmed?"

Zillah shook her head, "Rimlah *was* harmed though! He was covered in blood!"

Ednah smiled at her again and spoke softly, "Yes, he was covered in his own blood, but didn't you say that he didn't have a scratch on him when you cleaned him up?" Zillah's face showed that the truth was dawning on her. "Didn't some mysterious man in a gardener's cart bring him to your house and tell you that he had been healed of his wounds?"

Ednah let that sink in for a moment. "You see, Zillah, the Lord still cares about all of us, even if we do not acknowledge him the way we should. You see, even if you get angry with your father, he would still care for you."

Zillah was stunned by this revelation. She realized the night before that something miraculous had happened, but for some reason had chosen to ignore it. The simple truth Ednah was imparting to her so lovingly felt like a warm flood washing through her soul. Tears welled up in her eyes before she could stop them. She had to ask one more question before she lost her courage.

"Do you think that the Lord…" She couldn't think of another way to ask it that didn't sound childish, so she asked it the only way she could, "Does He love me?"

Ednah's eyes were so full of tears now that she could barely see as she emphatically answered, "Yes, Zillah. Even though you have not always acknowledged Him, He loves you very much. You are His child, after all!"

The two women embraced and cried with each other as if they were old friends. Mirah loved to give hugs, too, and was not about to miss this opportunity. The women looked down at the sweet child and laughed as they included her in their embrace.

At some point, Ednah looked up and saw Naamah standing at the bedroom door with a confused expression, "What's happening here?"

Chapter 21

THE WOMEN HAD FINISHED THEIR MEAL AFTER GETTING NAAMAH caught up on what had happened while she had been asleep. They were cleaning up when they heard the search party entering the yard.

Naamah excitedly burst through the door and into the darkness just as Tamari was being helped down from atop Nahla. Wailing sobs erupted as they met and clung to each other. "Thank you, Lord, for bringing her back to us! Thank you, Lord!" Naamah held her for as long as she could before Tamari groaned from the pressure of her vigorous squeeze.

When Bertlaw exited his carriage, he saw Zillah standing at the door with her arm around Ednah. "What has happened here?" he asked Rimlah, who was equally surprised by this strange sight.

Rimlah went to her and kissed her on the cheek. "Mother, I am sorry for the way I spoke to you before I left."

Zillah gave him a loving embrace. "It's alright son. I deserved it for the way I acted. Can you forgive me?"

"Of course, I can, Mother," Rimlah said with a smile. He couldn't remember the last time he saw her in such a relaxed and happy mood. Bertlaw came up next to him and noticed the same content look in her eyes. With his head cocked a bit sideways, exposing his curiosity, he asked, "It seems you had a good day, my dear."

Then, adding more surprise, Zillah leaned over, kissed Bertlaw on the cheek, and gently placed her hand on his face. "Yes, husband, I have. I have much to discuss with you on the way home tonight."

Bertlaw was happily confused. When he left that morning, Zillah was rude and surly. Now she seemed amiable, happy, and loving. "Of course, my dear. I look forward to it."

At this point, everyone gathered around the only available light, which was shining through the open front door. Enoch addressed Ednah first, "Ednah, the Lord told me we must gather in Urna tonight. We have been graciously invited to stay with Leader Bertlaw and his family."

Ednah was going to say something but was cut off by Mirah, who came bursting through the door, "Fader! Fader!" She ran and jumped at Enoch, who caught her in mid-air and threw her over his head with a proud smile and a hearty laugh. "There's my pretty girl! Did you miss me?"

"Yeaeaeaes," Mirah said in a silly sing-song.

He hugged her tight and put her down. She then noticed Tamari standing there and ran for her. "Tamawi!" she squealed as she flung her little arms around Tamari's legs.

Tamari bent down and hugged her tightly. "Hello, Mirah. It is very good to see you. I missed you so much since I saw you last. Did you miss me?"

Mirah answered in the same silly sing-song style, "Yeaeaeaes."

Mirah then noticed that she had an audience of several new faces smiling at her and admiring how cute she was. She was quite happy about this and enjoyed very much being the center of attention. She started to do a little dance and sing for them until Methuselah, seeing that his father wanted the floor right now, came over, grabbed her up, and whispered to her, "Shh, Mirah. Father needs to say something right now. Shh."

Thanking Methuselah with a simple nod, Enoch looked back to the group. "Alright. We will be ready to go shortly. Bertlaw, if you and your family would like to go ahead, Jaylon and I will travel together to Urna after we have gathered what we will need."

Bertlaw agreed and nodded to the captain, who started marshaling the soldiers in their marching formation. Zillah gave Ednah and Naamah one last hug before climbing into the carriage with help from Rimlah. They then rode out of sight.

Enoch looked to Jaylon. "Jaylon, do we need to go to your house for anything before we go?"

Jaylon looked at Naamah for her input. She shook her head. He looked back to Enoch. "No. I believe we have all we will need. When all this started, we sent Julis to stay with Naamah's sister. We will send word to her that everything is alright first thing tomorrow morning."

"Good then." Enoch looked at Mirah, "Little One, go get your favorite toy. We are going to stay in Urna tonight."

Methuselah put her down, and she replied as if it were a common occurrence, "Alwite." She then disappeared into the house to get the doll her mother had made her.

Next, Enoch looked to Methuselah, "Son, go get the cart from the barn and hook it up to the ox. We will have everyone ride it to the city."

"Yes, Father." Methuselah started toward the barn, looked around, and came to a sudden realization, "Father, where is Gardan?"

Enoch looked around and shook his head. "I don't know. Perhaps he went to Urna with Bertlaw when he left."

Methuselah shrugged his shoulders and continued toward the barn. Enoch walked to either side of the house to look for Gardan again. He was still nowhere in sight. "Gardan, where did you go?" he thought to himself.

Gardan was feeling very uncomfortable about the whole situation. He couldn't tell if he was scared or unsure of himself, out of place, or unworthy of the task. He felt as though the good people of Urna would be counting on him to fight this battle for them. At this moment, he felt woefully unable to provide the protection they needed.

"What protection can I give these people?" he thought as he made his way to a quiet place to think. He didn't really know where he was heading, but he had to get away and work all this out in his head. He felt terrible for sneaking away from the group the way he did. Still, he couldn't act brave any longer for fear that they, especially Enoch, would see through his façade. He didn't want to disappoint him but didn't want to give him any more false hopes either. He owed so much to Enoch, his very life, in fact.

True enough, Enoch had never said that he wanted him to fight against his wicked brothers and father, but who else was even capable of such a task? He knew what they were going to be up against. The city's soldiers had weapons for defense, but those young men had no idea what they would face. Those poor soldiers would be slaughtered.

He eventually came to the edge of a swampy area. The moon was not quite full, but his eyes had adjusted enough to the darkness to see a short distance into the swamp and make out the clumps of bulrushes that jutted out of the dark water. He sat down on a large rock and quietly listened to the chirping of the crickets and hoots of unseen owls.

He was awakened from his deep thoughts by the sound of Nahla scratching her backside against one of the massive cypress trees. He looked over at her and laughed to himself, "You don't seem too worried, my friend."

Then Leeno came near and started nudging his head against Gardan's legs, purring loudly to comfort him. He reached down and scratched his dark mane with a smile, "You don't seem too worried either, my loyal friend."

172

He soon resumed his deep thoughts and got lost in them until an idea came to him. He voiced his idea out loud in an attempt to feel less alone, "When Enoch struggles with things, he goes off by himself and prays to the Creator. Perhaps..." He cut that thought short with a shake of his head, "Enoch is a good and righteous man. The Creator listens to him, but why would He listen to anything *I* would ask? I am spawned from the evil of my father and wouldn't deserve a response from the God of Enoch."

Leeno nudged his legs and looked him in the eyes. Gardan studied his face for a moment, "What? Do you think I should try it anyway?" As if in response to what Gardan had said, Leeno gave him an almost stern expression and growled up at him.

"He did come to me in that dream before. Perhaps you are right, my furry friend." Leeno's expression brightened as he licked Gardan's hand and purred again. Gardan was astounded by the understanding that his feline friend seemed to show at times.

Gardan had never done this before and wasn't exactly sure how to start. After a few moments of trying to decide how to pray, he finally settled on just sitting where he was and looking up at the stars. Then he began.

"God of Enoch; Creator of all things; whatever You want to be called, I have never called on You before, and I'm not sure that You will even listen to one such as I. I know that I have not always been the kindest man. I also acknowledge that I was born from a father that knows nothing but evil. But I come to You and ask that You help me to protect these good people in Urna. I feel as though I am terribly weak in this role as protector, and I ask for You to speak to me. Please tell me what I should do. If not for me, then for Your faithful servant, Enoch."

He remained very still and continued looking into the night sky for several moments. He stayed very quiet, listening for the Creator's voice to rumble out of the atmosphere, but it didn't come. Finally, he took a deep breath and closed his eyes, shaking his head and feeling silly for thinking God would listen to him.

When he finally opened his eyes, they kept growing wider with surprise. All along the banks of the swamp, his answers lay before him. They were lined up as far as he could see on either side. He looked back to the night sky and cried with tears streaming down his face, "Thank You! Thank You!"

Chapter 22

Enoch, Jaylon, and their families had arrived in Urna late the night before and tried to get as much sleep as possible. However, the thought of what the next day would bring made restful sleep impossible. Ednah woke a little after sunrise to find she was alone in the beautifully furnished guestroom Zillah had provided them. She almost certainly knew where Enoch was. At a time like this, he would be praying and seeking God's direction in preparation for the coming day. However, she needed to find out where Mirah was.

She hurriedly got dressed and started her search. It didn't take long before she heard her joyously silly giggles coming from one of the rooms down a hallway. She followed the sound until she came to a room with a door ajar. She peered inside to see Tamari and Naamah sitting on the bed, braiding Mirah's hair and fussing over her. Mirah loved being fussed over like this and took full advantage of the opportunity with a beaming smile on her round little face.

Ednah gently pushed the door open. "I hope she didn't have you two up too early this morning."

Naamah looked up at Ednah with a giggle of her own, "Oh, Ednah, she's not bothering us a bit. Actually, we woke up pretty early this morning. We were talking and might have awakened Mirah with our laughter."

Tamari finished her masterpiece and took this opportunity to show off her work. "Go show your mother how pretty your hair looks," she whispered into Mirah's ear.

With that, Mirah jumped onto her feet and bounced along the soft bed as she walked to the end where her mother stood, "Look at my pretty hair!" She then twirled unsteadily to let her see the full view of her newly braided hair.

Ednah smiled brightly, "That's beautiful! You are such a pretty girl."

"Tank you," Mirah replied proudly as she flipped her tasseled locks with her hand.

Ednah bent down and kissed Mirah on the cheek before looking back to Naamah and Tamari, "Have either of you seen Enoch this morning?"

Naamah responded, "I haven't seen him this morning, but soon after Mirah came in, I think I might have heard someone go out the door."

Mirah piped up now, "Fadder woke me up dis morning. He was getting dwessed."

Ednah smiled at her, "Thank you, Mirah." She looked back to Naamah and Tamari, "I think I'll see if he's out on the garden patio."

She left the room, made her way to the patio door, and looked out to see if he was anywhere in sight. She quietly went out into the garden and saw Enoch in a secluded place with his hand on Jaylon's shoulder. Enoch was praying with him as Jaylon's shoulders shook with silent sobs.

It was times like this that made Ednah feel as if she were married to the most extraordinary man in the world. She smiled broadly, watched for a few moments, wiped away a few tears, and silently returned to the house to rejoin her friends in the bedroom.

Methuselah had slept fitfully. He actually felt as if he had not slept at all. He wasn't sure what time it was when he finally got up, but he was too restless to stay in bed any longer. He quietly got dressed, slipped out of the house, and decided to take a walk around the city.

He had been to the city many times before with his father to sell their vegetables to the vendors that gathered in the large city square near the main entrance. Still, he had never spent the night there before. Seeing the usually-bustling streets so quiet and tranquil felt odd to him. After a while, he started seeing a few people stirring around. Now, however, the sun was beginning to peek up over the surrounding hills, and the streets were quickly filling with the people, sounds, and smells he was used to encountering in the small metropolis of Urna.

As he wandered through the city, he could hear the excitement in the people's voices. Apparently, news traveled fast, even in a city as large as Urna. He stopped in the city square adjacent to the main entrance gate where the vendors were setting up their makeshift shops. He listened as they spoke among themselves about what they had heard.

A man selling melons spoke to another man who sold figs and olives, "I heard that Bertlaw rescued three girls from twenty giants down by the lake on his property, and that today the giants are coming to Urna to get their revenge!"

The other man responded, "No, it was one girl Bertlaw rescued from three giants, and one of the giants was captured and brought back with them."

Another man who had overheard this conversation then chimed in with his own version of events, "You are both confused. It wasn't Bertlaw who rescued anyone. It was Enoch who rescued the girl, and now he is going to lead the soldiers out to kill the giants. And there are seven giants, not twenty. But, one of them got scared and ran away."

"News travels fast, but not very accurately," he thought to himself. He heard several other versions of the story as he made his way through the square. Some were more accurate than others, but no one actually had the story straight. He found it somewhat amusing how so many people had so many versions of the same story so wrong. Methuselah wanted to step in and correct them all but decided to just walk away and let them continue to argue amongst themselves.

Eventually, he left the square and could hear the sound of swords clashing against shields. He followed the din and found the training facility where the soldiers were sparing with each other, practicing their skills. He found it fascinating how they moved and parried each other's advances with so much grace and ease of motion. It was almost like a dance, a very deadly dance.

He found himself a good place to sit and watch the proceedings on some stairs leading up to a platform that overlooked the entire complex. As he sat watching, mesmerized by the flashing of metal in the morning sun, he was suddenly jarred by a commanding voice, "What do you think of them?"

Methuselah jumped to his feet and quickly turned to see who was speaking. "Oh! I'm sorry. I didn't know you had come up behind me."

"I apologize for startling you Methuselah," said the captain.

Methuselah's pulse settled, and he thought for a moment about what the captain had asked him, "They are impressive. The way they anticipate each other's moves and calmly deflect the other's attacks is truly remarkable. They must train a lot to be this good at it."

The captain took a deep breath and slowly released it with a masculine sigh. "They do train a great deal. These men have come a long way since I started training them." He paused momentarily, continuing, "I am concerned for them, however."

Methuselah looked at him inquisitively and started to ask him what he meant, but the captain saw the question before it was asked, "Methuselah, they are very skilled at sparing with each other, but they have never had to go into any real battle situations before. As impressive as they may appear, they are, as yet, untested."

Methuselah looked back to where the soldiers were training and thought about what the captain had said. "I suppose fighting against each other is a lot different than fighting men the size of Gardan."

"Yes. It is very different," replied the captain in a very solemn and thoughtful voice. "I have become very close to these men over the years that I have been training them. I know each of their names, the names of their wives, and the names of their children. They have become like my own children, and I suppose I'm worried that they could be killed today. I guess, in that way, I am *also* untested."

Methuselah could hear the caring in this valiant man's voice. He had already thought a great deal of him but was even more awed by his concern for his men's wellbeing. He searched his mind for a word of encouragement before commenting, "Captain, you have done very well in training your men. You seem to have taught them everything they need to know to keep them stay alive in a battle. What else could you have done?"

The captain thought about that for a moment, "I suppose that is all I can do." The captain laughed and looked at Methuselah, "You have your father's wisdom, Methuselah. What else would your father say to make me feel better about this whole situation right now?"

Methuselah responded without hesitation, "He would say that you have done all that you can do. Now, you should put the rest in the hands of the Creator. He would say that as much as you feel like those soldiers are your children, the Lord created each of them and loves them even more than you do. My father would tell you to humble yourself before the Creator and ask His protection on each of your men. At least, I think that is what my father would say."

"That is very good, my son," came Enoch's voice from around the platform's corner. "That is exactly what I would say." Enoch laughed heartily at the surprised expressions staring back at him when he came into view.

Methuselah smiled derisively at him. "I suppose you think that was funny, Father."

Enoch was still laughing as the captain put a firm hand on Enoch's shoulder, "You would make a good spy, Enoch. You move very quietly."

"It wasn't very difficult really. You were so busy listening to my sage advice through my son here that you weren't aware of the real thing in your midst," Enoch said.

The captain nodded his agreement, "Once again, I believe you are right."

Enoch turned his attention back to Methuselah, "You left Bertlaw's house very early this morning. You should have left word where you were going. Your mother will be worried about you. You should probably get back there and let her know you are alright."

Methuselah nodded and turned back to the captain, "It was good to talk to you, Sir."

"Likewise, my astute young friend." The captain watched as Methuselah walked away. Turning to Enoch, the Captain continued, "You have a brilliant boy there."

Enoch was also watching after him. "Yes, he is. I am quite proud of him." He took a deep breath and shook his head with a half-hearted smile. "At least I am usually quite proud of him. There are times when I'm not sure what he is thinking, but I suppose it is always that way with your children."

"That is true," said the captain. "I can tell you that my father wondered the same things about me when I was his age."

After a moment of silence, the captain changed the subject to what was truly on his mind, "So, what do you think this day shall bring us, Enoch?"

"Victory," was his one-word answer. "The Lord told me He would show us His love and power today. He has never failed to do what He said He would do before, and I do not believe He will fail to do so today."

The captain searched Enoch's face for any sign of doubt but found none. "I wish I could have as much faith as you. I have never been around anyone who puts so much trust in the Creator as you, Enoch. Where does all that blind faith come from? Going up that mountain yesterday the way you did, without even so much as a weapon… I cannot imagine that. I cannot imagine what must have been going through your mind."

Enoch gave him a caring smile. "Captain, my faith *is* my weapon. My Lord is my shield. Nothing can harm me without His approval. You see, the Lord not only created everything, but He also controls everything. There is nothing that happens that He does not already know about beforehand. He knows what will happen before it even occurs because He sees time, not the way we do, but from beginning to end at the same time. He promised us the victory yesterday because He has already seen it." Enoch paused and put a hand on the captain's shoulder, "You see, my friend; we have already won the day."

Enoch let that sink in for a moment before moving on, "Captain, you are a good and noble man. The Creator made you that way. He also made you with a place in your heart for Himself. He wants you to ask Him to give you the faith you say you lack. With that faith will come a higher purpose for your life, a more fulfilling life." Enoch could see the truth of what he was saying starting to open the captain's heart. "I ask you, Captain, will you allow the Creator, who loves you very much and wants a relationship with you like He has with me, to fill that empty place in your heart?"

The captain looked uncomfortable and stammered for a moment. He felt like he was torn inside. He knew Enoch was speaking the truth to him, but something inside him resisted. Finally, after what he thought was an eternity without speaking, his mind formulated an answer, "Enoch, what you say is compelling, but I am a man of action. I trust in myself and my training. I just don't see how I can put my trust in a God I have not yet seen." Feeling very uncomfortable and no longer wanting to look Enoch in the eye, he turned to walk away. He stopped a few cubits away and, only half turning back, added, "Ask me again after this great victory the Lord is supposed to bring us today."

Enoch was saddened for him and said a silent prayer as he walked back to Bertlaw's house. Quietly and invisibly, the Lord walked along with him.

Chapter 23

THE EARTHBOUND MONSTERS AND THEIR ANGRY LITTLE FATHER were finally released from their unseen snares and stumbled to their feet. They had spent the entire night sleeping on the ground, their feet still stuck solidly to the earth where they stood the day before. None of them had slept well, not only because of the hard ground but also because of Syclah's incessant moaning and wailing over his severely injured ankle.

Azazel was now irately brushing the soil off his clothes and muttering as he had done all night. The five brothers were also angry but kept their anger to themselves, giving their father a chance to rant without interruption. Without being told, they started gathering their swords and readying themselves for the revenge they had been thinking about since yesterday.

More out of the pleasure of giving an order than the need to give it, Azazel barked, "Prepare yourselves! We shall destroy Urna and all her people today for what was done to us!" Then, more to himself than to his sons, "Today Enoch *dies!*"

Enoch had spent most of the morning in deep prayer and supplication for the people of Urna. He walked the entire circumference of the city, following the mostly-built walls as he went.

The captain had seen fit to post soldiers at every part of the wall that was yet unfinished, and Enoch put a hand on the shoulder of each one, saying a prayer for them as he passed by.

Halfway around the third time, he suddenly realized the Lord was beside him. "Oh!" he cried as he fell prostrate to the ground. "Forgive me, Lord, for not seeing You before now!"

The Lord smiled at him lovingly. "Stand up Enoch. There is no need to forgive you for not seeing Me. I only now revealed Myself to you. I have been listening to your prayers and have enjoyed hearing the way you care for all of My children. The prayers of a faithful and righteous man are sweet to My ears."

Enoch stood to his feet, "Thank You, my Lord."

The Creator continued, "Enoch, I have released Azazel and his sons from the snare I made for them. They are making their way to Urna now. I want you to go to the main gate of the city and stand on the wall. Tell the people that I want them to remain within the walls of the city if they want to live. Tell the soldiers to keep their swords sheathed, stay where they are, and do not advance against the giants. Tell them that, if they will only be still and trust Me to deliver them, they will all live. But, if the people of Urna go outside the city gate, or if the soldiers attempt to advance against the giants, they shall die."

Enoch bowed and answered the Lord's request, "As You say, I will do." He paused for a moment, wanting to ask a question of the Creator, but the Lord knew his question before it could be asked.

"Gardan will be alright. He was feeling underequipped for the task ahead of him, but I have given him new strength. I shall show My glory and power through him. He is a special creation all to himself. He was born of evil, but I shall use him for good. In fact, his soul has more goodness in it than most of the people who call out to Me when they are in need."

Enoch was happy to hear the Lord speaking highly of his large friend. "Thank You, my Lord. I have been greatly blessed to have Gardan in my life. He truly has been a good friend to me."

"Now," said the Lord, "Do not waste any time getting to the gate of the city. Deliver My message just as I told you to, and trust in Me."

"Yes, my Lord." With that, Enoch went quickly on his way.

Although Bertlaw, Jaylon, Rimlah, and Methuselah had asked them to stay at the house, the women insisted on going to the city gate to see what would happen when the enemy arrived. Ednah, however, had smartly decided to leave Mirah with Zillah's servants, who were more than happy to look after her. The group made their way through the seemingly empty streets. Everyone in the city appeared to be gathered at the gates to see the spectacle. As they neared the city square, their suspicions were confirmed.

Given how the people acted, it almost seemed like a party was about to occur. Throngs of people crowded the square and jockeyed for the best position to see the day's entertainment unfold. Vendors were selling trinkets and sweet treats while the men who usually ran the gambling tables were collecting bets, wagering whether the giants could defeat the soldiers. This with no apparent regard for what that would mean for their own survival or the people wagering with them. Methuselah was astounded at their behavior. It seemed to him that they were either completely unaware or utterly unconcerned about the potential danger of the situation.

They pushed their way through the crowd, past the musicians and dancing girls, and around the food vendors to where the captain stood with his soldiers guarding the gate, trying their best to keep the citizens from venturing outside.

"Captain," said Methuselah while scanning the boisterous crowds. "What are all these people doing here? Do they not realize the danger they may be in?"

The captain eyed him, Bertlaw, Rimlah, and Jaylon, then the women accompanying them with an expression of unbelief at the question he asked. "Are *you* not concerned for the safety of these women you brought with *you*?"

Methuselah and Jaylon looked back at the women, then at each other. He looked back at the captain with a sheepish grin and shrugged, "They insisted on coming."

The captain only gave him a knowing grin and turned his attention back through the gate to scan the horizon for the enemy just in time to see an excited Enoch come around the corner of the wall and into the gate.

"Captain," said a breathless Enoch. "I need to get on top of the wall to give a message to the people of Urna! The giants are on their way and the Creator has told me to give them instructions as to what they should do."

The captain eyed him momentarily and then nodded, "This way. A staircase takes you to the top of the gate."

As the captain led the way, Enoch acknowledged Methuselah, Bertlaw, Rimlah, and Jaylon with firm hands on their shoulders and then gave Ednah a quick kiss. He then followed the captain through a doorway in the wall.

Per the captain's instructions, he followed the dark stairway until he emerged into the sunlight again and found he could look out over the crowd. He put his hands up in the air and waved them furiously to get the attention of the people milling about below him. Only a few of them even noticed, pointing at him and laughing. He tried to yell but to no avail. He couldn't be heard over the din of the music and merry-making. He didn't know what else to do to get their attention and prayed to the Lord to be heard.

Just then, an enormously loud, almost deafening, crack of lightning crashed behind him. All at once, the crowd got very quiet and looked to see where the noise had come from. All eyes were now on Enoch. He silently thanked the Lord and took the opportunity.

"People of Urna, many of you know me and know that I speak with the Creator! He has given me a message of instruction for you." Most people looked at each other, muttering amongst themselves before returning their gaze to the strange man, curious about what he was saying.

Enoch continued, "This is what the Sovereign Lord says! The enemy comes soon. If you want to live through the day, you must follow His instructions! He says not to listen to what the enemy says. Do not go outside the gates of the city. You are to stay within the gates and trust Him to deliver you from harm. He will show His love for you and keep you safe if you only do what He says. However, if you go outside the city gate, you will surely die! If you do what the enemy urges you to do, you will be destroyed. You are to trust in the Lord, your God, to deliver you from danger. He loves each of you and wants to show you that He cares for you. Only, you must do as He says."

A collective gasp came over the crowd as they looked through the gate out into the open field. Enoch saw their reaction and followed their pointing fingers. As he turned, he saw Azazel and his five evil sons lined up side by side, moving toward the gate. When they had come to within about two hundred cubits of the city, Azazel put up a hand, and they stopped.

Azazel put his hand down and eyed the little man atop the city wall with complete disdain. "Enoch!" he muttered to himself through clenched teeth. He felt as if he had waited for an eon for the opportunity to exact revenge on this man at his master's request. He could feel the excitement of this moment running coldly through his veins. This impudent man who had dared to teach the stupid little people to read so they could know the will of the Creator was finally going to pay for his insolence. He whispered to himself, "Today, Enoch will bow to the will of Lucifer! He will do this in front of all these people so that they will know the true master of this world!"

Seeing that Enoch was elevated above the puny people of the city and not wanting to be outdone, he scanned the area to find something to stand on. He saw a large boulder across the field and barked an order to Harclah. "Go get that boulder and bring it here!"

Without a word, Harclah went over and picked up the massive boulder, easily carried it over, and dropped it down next to Azazel. A gasp of astonishment went up collectively from within the city. Azazel smiled at this. He could taste the fear from where he was.

He barked another order to Harclah, "Put me up on top of the boulder so that these little rats can hear what I say!" Harclah obeyed.

"People of Urna, hear what I, Azazel, have to say! I am here for one man. There is no need for bloodshed. If you give me Enoch, I will be on my way without any more trouble. Send him out to me and you will all live." Azazel waited for the response.

The people started murmuring to each other and soon turned their attention to the strange man on the wall. The captain could see where this was leading, grabbed five of his soldiers, and stood guard at the doorway leading to the top of the wall. The crowd started moving toward them until he and his soldiers drew their swords and wielded them menacingly as a warning.

Someone in the crowd spoke up, "Captain, you saw for your-self what just one of those giants can do! Why should we all die because of this one man?" The rest of the throng echoed their agreement threateningly. "For the good of the city, let's give him what he wants!" Cheers went up from the crowd.

The lightning cracked again, getting the attention of the crowd once more. Enoch yelled at them as loudly as he could, "Trust in the Lord, your God! The Creator of all things will deliver us from this man's threats if you only trust in Him! He loves you all and will keep you from harm, but only if you follow what He has said." There was more murmuring from the crowd.

Azazel could hear all that Enoch was telling the people and was furious. His anger burned inside him. He could not believe the audacity these people were showing. He calmed himself before speaking again.

"This man, Enoch, is doing you people a great disservice with his lies! Who is *he* that he would know the will of God? He tells you that if you listen to me you will die, but the truth is that he is only interested in his own safety." He could sense that he was getting through to them.

"To show you that I am a reasonable man, I will give you another option. I am not going to leave until I get Enoch. So, if you will not send him out to me, then all of you may come out here where you will be safe while we go in after him. If not, then I will have no other choice but to destroy your city and all of you with it! Those are your *only* choices! I suggest you choose wisely."

The crowd started to murmur again, and Enoch watched with horror as many of them started making their way toward the gate. The captain had his own doubts about all of this but had to make a decision. He could see that their options were few and that, realistically, a good case for following Azazel's advice could be made. However, deep down in his gut, he knew Enoch was right. He made his choice and yelled to the soldiers who were still at the gate, "Hold the gate! No one leaves the city!"

To a man, the soldiers were also confused about what they should do. They were as scared as the rest of the crowd but had also seen what Enoch had done the day before. Most of them decided to follow orders and drew their swords to ward off the pressing crowd, but a few chose to do what Azazel wanted. They turned and walked out the gate, opening up a path for hundreds of people to filter out with them.

Enoch felt sick as he watched a third of the crowd marching to their deaths. "Come back! You must stay in the city to be saved! Azazel is lying to you!" But they only cursed him as they walked through the gate and gathered outside. They congregated atop a slight rise so they could be spectators to the killing of the fools left inside. The rest of the people who stayed within the city walls were unsure of their decisions but also knew Enoch was a good man who had always spoken the truth. He may be somewhat strange, but he was also known to be the wisest man in the area.

Azazel watched with glee as the crowd made their way out of the gate. However, his delight turned back to anger when he saw that only about a third of the city's people had followed his advice.

"Do the rest of you wish to die today? Surely, you people do not doubt that I will destroy you!" He waited for a response, but his anger burned in his eyes when no more people came out. He turned to Beodan and spoke so that none of the people outside the gate could hear him, "Beodan, kill all these people who have come out of the city! I want the people inside the city to know fear today."

Without a word, and faster than the eyes could follow, Beodan flashed by the crowd gathered outside and back to his father's side with a bloody sword in hand. In one pass, Beodan had taken the heads, which were only now falling to the ground, from the entire group of foolish souls on the rise.

The people left inside the gate were shocked at what they had just witnessed. Some of the women screamed in horror, while others were too mortified to make a sound and stood with their hands over their mouths. The men of the city only stared with their mouths agape trying not to show the fear that made their every nerve tingle. To most, this was the most gruesome thing they had ever witnessed.

Tears streaming down his face, Enoch turned from the spectacle and, once again, addressed the remaining crowd, "The Lord warned them not to go out of the city, but they would not listen. Please, stay inside the walls and let the Lord protect you. He has promised that if you do what He said, He will show you His love. He will deliver you from danger." This time, instead of murmuring, there were only muffled sobs and a few nods of agreement.

Methuselah found himself on his knees after seeing the tragedy unfold before him. His legs had gotten wobbly and gave out underneath him. He noticed after a few moments that He had Tamari's hand in his own and looked over to see the tears rolling down her cheeks. There was only one thought in his mind, and he spoke it to her, "We need to pray."

Tamari looked at him and nodded her agreement. They prayed fervently for the remaining people's safety, that the Creator would show his love and mercy, and that the people would be more willing to trust in the Lord from this point forward.

Enoch watched from above and saw that Methuselah and Tamari were on their knees praying. However, what impressed him most was that the people around them started falling to their knees to do the same. It didn't take long before everyone else within the city gate, including the captain and his remaining soldiers, followed suit. To Enoch, this was a beautiful sight to behold. He raised his hands to the sky and praised God for what He was about to do.

***

Azazel watched with amazement at what was happening in the city. This was not at all what he expected. He expected bedlam, hysteria, panic, screaming, crying, and begging for his mercy, but praying?

He paced back and forth atop his perch, seething with rage and muttering to himself. He was utterly at a loss to explain this reaction. Any other time he and his motley crew had laid siege to a city, the people could always be counted on to react with panicked fear. He had seen them run for their lives. He had seen them try to hide. He had seen them try foolishly to fight back. He had even seen a few of them kill themselves in an attempt to cheat him out of the pleasure. But this was new.

Skaldan watched the praying people with some curiosity. He found it to be confusing and downright silly. He laughed at the sight of these puny people calling out to God. "Father, why does the Creator care for these weak creatures? Why would He even waste His love on them? Are they not useless?"

Azazel answered through gritted teeth, "*Yes*, they are useless! And *yes*, they are weak! It is time to show them just how useless and weak they are!"

Chapter 24

"KILL THEM ALL!" SHOUTED AZAZEL. THE EVIL CLAN BEGAN marching toward the gate of Urna. The ground shook with the footfalls of the massive men as Azazel watched from the safety of his rocky perch.

He trembled with delight as his freakish sons approached the gate, but something didn't feel right to him. As they got further away from him, the ground seemed to shake with more and more intensity. Also, the quaking didn't match up with their footfalls the way it should have. There was something else happening here.

The five hulking giants also noticed that something was wrong. They stopped their march and turned back to their father to see if he was feeling the same thing, only to find him looking just as confused.

Azazel began to look around to find the source of the disturbance. He looked to his right; nothing. He looked behind him; nothing. He looked to his left; nothing. Then again, what was that? He could see the tops of the trees in the distance shaking violently in a wave that seemed to be coming closer and closer in their direction. His sons followed his eyes and saw the same disturbance in the trees.

When Enoch heard Azazel give the attack order, he didn't even open his eyes. He just stayed quiet as the Lord whispered in his ear, "Be still. Your deliverance is at hand." Enoch thanked the Creator for being so faithful to His word, and only then did he open his eyes.

Enoch saw the evil giants marching toward the city. Then he saw them stop and look around, confused by something. At this point, he heard and felt the rumbling from the forest to his right. He saw that Azazel and his sons were looking in that direction and followed suit. From his vantage point, Enoch could plainly see the trees quaking and that whatever was making them do so was heading his way. He wondered if the Lord had sent a flood to wash the enemy away, but instantly realized that a flood would also wash away the people of Urna, who the Lord promised to deliver.

At that moment, thirty of the largest, fastest, and meanest-looking leviathans Enoch had ever seen were spewing forth from the forest's edge. He was astounded as he beheld the wondrous sight. Adding to his amazement was the fact that every one of them had a blazingly white heavenly warrior riding atop with his brilliantly flashing sword drawn. Nahla, with her enormous rider, accompanied by Leeno, who strode regally alongside, crashed out of the forest after them.

Only Enoch could see the heavenly warriors atop the beasts, but the sight was breathtaking just the same. When the people of Urna saw this amazing sight, they all jumped to their feet, and some cheered, "The Lord has delivered us!" Others just watched the fantastic spectacle take place as if it were a dream.

Methuselah, Tamari, Ednah, and Jaylon all threw their hands in the air to give glory to the Lord, who had provided their deliverance from what would have been sure death. Bertlaw, Rimlah, and Zillah, who weren't quite sure what to say, just stood there, wide-eyed and stunned at what they were witnessing.

When Azazel saw the fearsome tide of leviathan crash through the edge of the forest, he stood limp, glad to be atop his rocky island and out of reach of all those jagged teeth. He could see their riders clearly and let out a loud whimpering scream, "No!" He sounded like a petulant child who just had his favorite toy taken away. When he saw the behemoth and its rider come out behind them, his eyes narrowed, and the anger burned within him as he whispered through clenched teeth, "Gardan!"

Beodah was the first to meet his end. Not as swift as his brother and clumsier on dry land than in water, he swung inelegantly at the first leviathan to approach him. His sword sent sparks and fractured bronze flying in all directions as it shattered against the hard scales of the beast. It was too late for him to do anything else, for the monstrous lizard had already taken his arm as another snapped him in two with ease.

The next was Syclah. He couldn't move very well with his injured ankle and was relegated to swatting at them as they attacked from four directions. He was able to knock the first two aside, but the third spewed a blistering stream of fire in his face, knocking him down, while the fourth was able to snap down on his flailing legs and take them off at the hip. He had no chance as the first two returned to finish the job.

Harclah had managed to use his unmatched strength to get one of the creatures by the tail and was using him to bat away the others, but that didn't last long. One of the great beasts was able to get behind him and took off one of his legs. Without any balance, he quickly became easier prey and was dispatched in moments.

Beodan was fast enough to dart and dive out of the way of the leviathans for a while but was starting to tire. As his brothers were taken out, more of the creatures were freed up to help with him. It was only a matter of time before he would meet his fate.

As he realized his only option now was to run, he turned and darted headlong into the waiting jaws of another of the fearsome lizards. It was over before he knew what hit him.

Skaldan, though not as bright as Gardan, was more intelligent than the rest. He quickly deduced that his best and only option was to get up on the boulder where his fear-struck father was hiding. He watched with horror as his brothers were gruesomely dispatched one by one. Now, the creatures congregated at the base of his perch, jaws snapping and fire-belching as they lunged upward but not quite being able to reach him. They were, however, able to singe him a bit. He let out yelps and hopped about, continually attempting to pat himself out as the flames climbed his now hairless legs.

Gardan laughed heartily at him as he dismounted Nahla and walked confidently up amidst the throng of fierce and anxious beasts, "I remember you saying I was weak and stupid for befriending the animals, Brother. Well, who is the weak one now, Skaldan?" He couldn't help but laugh again at the frightened look on the faces of his brother and father. "And you, Father. You loved to pit us against each other so that we could satisfy your insatiable thirst for blood. I regretted for years that I didn't kill you when I had the chance, but now I am glad I didn't. If I had killed you then, I wouldn't be able to watch you squirm like the scared little worm you are."

Azazel tried to use his most appeasing voice as he pleaded with Gardan, "My son, I only wanted you to be strong enough to survive in a world as harsh as this one can be. What I did, I did out of concern for you. I can see now that I was wrong. You have become a very strong man that I would be proud to call my son. I was very worried about you when you left. I am so glad that you are alright. I…"

Gardan had heard all he wanted to hear from this slimy little man, "*Enough!* You have never been concerned with anyone but yourself! You are an evil little man and you raised evil sons. The only love I ever got as a child was from my mother, and when Syclah killed her, you only snickered and told me to stop my sniveling. You fully deserve what you are about to receive!"

Skaldan saw that his father's attempts at appeasement were getting him nowhere and decided on another approach, "Gardan, if you want revenge against us, you have it. But, if watching four of our brothers die horrible deaths is not enough for you, I don't think watching Father and I die the same way will satisfy you either. It must come through your own hands if you truly want your revenge. Send these creatures away, and I will grant you your chance at the revenge you want."

Gardan thought about that for a moment. It was true that what he really wanted was to kill Skaldan with his bare hands. His brother had tortured him since his earliest memories, and he had never been able to get the satisfaction of revenge. But his heart was different now. It wasn't payback that he wanted now. It was the satisfaction that comes from doing what is right that Gardan wanted now. Ever since he had prayed to the Creator the night before, his heart felt clean for the first time in his miserable life, and he wanted it to stay that way.

Gardan eyed his brother with pity for his soul, "Skaldan, I don't want revenge anymore. I will admit, that's what I wanted for many years, but now I just want you to leave these good people alone. Father has told you many lies about them. They are not 'worthless rats,' as he calls them, and they did not steal his birthright or those of his brothers in heaven. They were created for one reason; to give praise to the Creator. Father and his brothers were created to serve the Creator, but they threw that all away for their own self interests. Now they go around corrupting these poor people, trying to mislead them. Brother, you don't have to do it anymore. You can walk away from all of that as I have if you truly want to. But, for now I will be satisfied if you would just go away and leave these poor people alone."

Azazel looked at Skaldan and gave him a wicked look, and then looked back to Gardan, "We will leave and never come back if you would only call off these beasts. You have our word."

Gardan eyed him suspiciously and then relented, "Alright, then." He turned and whistled at the giant lizards. Immediately, they turned from their prey and started back toward the forest from which they had come. Skaldan and Azazel could not help but be impressed at the way with which Gardan was able to communicate with the creatures.

As the last of them disappeared into the tree line, Skaldan slid down the side of the rock and helped his father down. Gardan watched them carefully as they did so. "Alright, Father, you gave your word that you will leave and never bother these people again. For once, keep your word."

Azazel nodded and turned to walk away, with Skaldan following suit. Gardan watched for a moment as they took their first steps to leave. He then turned back toward the city where his new friends awaited him.

He took two steps before there was a shout, "Gardan, look out behind you!" As he turned to look, he saw Skaldan closing the gap between them, sword high, and thrusting it toward him. He was too late to stop it! He didn't have time to get out of the way of the bronze missile. It was going to plunge right into his chest.

Suddenly, at the last possible moment, there was a dark brown and bronze flash across his eyes. It took a few moments for Gardan to realize what had happened. Then, the weight of the situation hit him. Leeno, his closest friend in the world, had taken the sword meant for him. There, on the ground between Gardan and a stunned Skaldan, lay the impaled body of the lion, sword still in place.

The rage within Gardan came to the surface with an eruption that Skaldan was unprepared for. Before Skaldan could react, the light of day blinked out. His vision returned to him just in time to see four huge knuckles fill his view. The daylight blinked out again. He came to again, just long enough to comprehend that he was sprawled out on the ground with Gardan on top of him and his head in a vice-like grip from either side. Gardan looked at him eye to eye with a ferocious countenance. "You will never kill anyone ever again!" Then, with a quick twist of the head and a loud crack of the neck, it was over. The wicked, black light in Skaldan's eyes faded and disappeared forever.

Gardan staggered to his feet and looked up to see where his father was, only in time to see a cloud of black smoke where he once stood. He scanned the horizon from one side to the other but to no avail. His cowardly father was gone. He had seen his father do this only once before, when he was trapped and without any other options. Gardan thought his father was only doing what a true coward would do when it was time to pay for his crimes; run.

He then turned his attention to his old feline companion. He walked over, dropped to his knees, buried his face in Leeno's mane, and sobbed for his best friend.

Enoch and Methuselah approached the quivering giant with flowing tears of their own, placing caring hands upon his back. They cried with their friend, sharing his loss and letting him know he was not alone. This went on for a long while. No one said a word.

After some time, Gardan sat up and wiped his eyes. He gently pulled the sword from his limp friend and scooped him up. He then spoke in a sad and unsteady voice, "Nahla and I need to be alone with our friend for a while." With that, he walked away, Nahla following closely, her head down and tail dragging sorrowfully behind her.

After watching their huge friend walk away, Methuselah and Enoch walked together back to the gate of Urna, where their family and friends were waiting. They all took time to embrace each other and tell each other they were loved. After seeing so much death, it seemed like the thing to do.

The captain watched all this with great interest. He was feeling his own losses today. Thirty of his soldiers had chosen to go outside the gate and now lay in a heap atop the low hill. He tried to hide it, but tears flowed easily down his cheeks.

A voice from behind him got his attention. "Captain, I am sorry for your losses today. I know you cared deeply for them." The captain turned to see Enoch.

"I guess you were right about everything you said today. There is a lot that I don't understand about your faith in the Creator, but I can see the truth in it." He took a deep breath before continuing, "Could we talk about it for a while? I believe I need to get some things settled between the Lord and me."

Enoch smiled widely. "Yes, my friend. We can talk about it as long as you want."

<hr />

Azazel had disappeared in a puff of smoke. He could have done it at any point he wanted but thought he would wait until it was absolutely necessary, just in case he could still see his plan through. If he was determined before to see Enoch dead, he was now obsessed with the idea.

"I *will* kill you, Enoch!" he muttered to himself. "You can count on it!"

As he walked down a wooded path, he saw that another trail to his left led to an opening where he could make out the skyline of an unwalled city to which he had never been. "This shows promise," he said as he came toward the opening in the path.

Suddenly, there before him was an enormous Lion with an ugly gash clearly visible on His back. His eyes had an angry red glow, and He roared menacingly as if to block the way. Azazel knew full well who this Lion was. He threw his hands up submissively and decided to go somewhere else for now.

"Perhaps I will see what the rest of my children are doing in the north," he said as he vanished into the forest.

To order additional copies of

Giants in the Earth;
The Methuselah Chronicles

visit www.amazon.com

CPSIA information can be obtained
at www.ICGtesting.com
Printed in the USA
LVHW051642140523
746958LV00015B/1555